Dr. Chaim V. Melamed

22
STORIES AROUND THE GLOBE*
*AND WHAT THEY TELL US ABOUT LIFE

Dr. Chaim V. Melamed

22

STORIES AROUND THE GLOBE*

*AND WHAT THEY TELL US ABOUT LIFE

Translated by Rachel K.
www.Trans-that.com

Graphic Design: Bat Chen Nachmani
Cover Photo: Andrei Mihalcea, dreamstime
Printed in Israel 2013

KIP – Kotarim International Publishing LTD
Publisher: Moshe Alon
Kip@smile.net.il

Dr. Chaim V. Melamed

22

STORIES AROUND THE GLOBE*

*AND WHAT THEY TELL US ABOUT LIFE

The Stories and the Places

Dedicated to Naomi my love

About the book and the stories

Our lives are a collection of stories.
The great majority of these stories form part of our routine, but a select few are fortuitous stories with a momentous impact on our life, development, future, and sometimes even... our past. These stories are the result of astounding coincidences, rare incidents, unbelievable situations, amazing encounters, at times blurring the distinction between imaginary and real, between the actual and the virtual world.

The twenty two stories that I have chosen to present in this book represent 'unique' incidents that occurred in various parts of the world and had a dramatic effect on the lives of their characters. Each story concludes with a short message, providing food for thought and sometimes a practical lesson.

These outstanding stories have another worthwhile benefit: Using imagination, they take us to distant places that are fascinating, magical and enchanting, unknown and unheard of, different and strange.
The stories invite their readers to join them in a journey to countries such as India, Georgia, Burma (Myanmar) and Mexico, as well as Australia, Japan, South Africa, Brazil, and the Caribbean Islands. Other pleasing and interesting cities included are: New York, Copenhagen, Granada, Nashville, London, Toronto, Lille, Salvador, Wiesbaden, Prague, Tel Aviv, and more...

For me this book has personal significance, as it is my eleventh published book. It commences my second decade of literary activity.
I must admit that I wrote this book mostly thanks to the enthusiastic support and encouragement of my readers (in English and Hebrew) who send me constant feedback and supply me with energy for my next project.

Every storyteller is supported by a life partner who provides stories and insights. My partner and the love of my life is Naomi. She is with me both in these stories and in the stories of our life. Like me, it is not always easy for her to distinguish between actual occurrences and imaginary events that occur to the various characters in my stories.

Naomi, thank you from the bottom of my heart, with a hug full of attachment.

I hope you have an enjoyable experience (just as I myself enjoyed writing each of the following 22 stories). Once again, I would appreciate your feedback… in any language!

The author
chaim_m@walla.co.il

1

The young guitarist at Alhambra and the elderly nurse from Tennessee

● ● ●

Spain was suffering from a high level of unemployment, perhaps prompting the firm attitude of the police towards street performers that spring. The men in uniform waged a constant battle against young people who congregated in the city center, and also banished the musicians and jugglers from Granada's impressive squares and streets, in a city whose beauty was only enhanced by its many historical and religious vicissitudes.

It was an intriguing date, the first of April. On this specific day the tourists in Granada were mostly groups of retirees, taking advantage of their free time, free will, and free (or freed) resources to realize their dream of seeing the world.

Southern Spain was enjoying an early spring, engulfed by American tourists. They loved to visit the fascinating ancient colorful region of Andalusia. It was only natural for tourist itineraries in this region to include a visit to Alhambra Hill, towering over the city's environs. The best known attraction in this popular complex is the magnificent castle of Alcazaba. The impressive external architectural beauty and internal wealth and design of this building cannot be exaggerated. It is indeed a must-see tourist attraction. The castle is surrounded by manicured gardens combining fine landscaping, lush greenery, and rivulets crossed by small narrow miniature bridges.

At this pleasant, warm moment, Steve Bull, a main character in this story and one of the street performers who had decided to relocate from the city center to more distant locations, was stationed on one of these bridges. He was a young man, 25 years old, with a knack for playing familiar and pleasing melodies on his guitar. Sometimes his music showed signs of real talent. At such times it was evident that he could have performed at the most exclusive concert halls. Indeed he could have, but the full potential of his talent had never ripened. Until this day his life had been completely wasted. He had had the opportunity to hit it big but this did not happen, mainly his own fault in addition to a lack of good fortune.

It was the tourists who had prompted the young American to come and play his guitar on the bridge facing the castle. He played for many hours. Euro coins thrown by tourists who enjoyed his music and rewarded him with a tip, either large or small, landed from time to time in his open guitar case. Occasionally their appreciation for his music generated foreign or local bills. Tall skinny stooped Steve somehow managed to survive the days and nights, with hardly a penny to his name. His wild unkempt hair and thick beard had kept him company for the past two years, as he travelled with his guitar throughout Europe. His ragged hippie look, red eyes, worn out clothes, and the tattoos that covered every visible part of his body, gave no sign of the great hopes his friends and family had had for him only a few short years ago. Even the case in which he kept his guitar, the instrument that was his entire world and his anchor, looked like something he had found in a garbage can and matched his appearance and his wasted life, the life of a star who had lost his way.

His current life showed no hint of the expectations he had aroused in everyone who had known him during his studies at the University of California in Berkeley. Only three years ago he had been considered a musical genius – as a musician and a composer. At the young age of 14 he had won second prize in California's Musical Star, a prestigious competition for young musicians. At Berkeley he had been a real star, both as a musician and as a student in the Faculty of Mathematics. Mathematics and music were closely linked for him.

But three years ago most everything in Steve's life had gone wrong. His long-time girlfriend had left him. His parents had abandoned him, and the subsequent plunge in his studies in both fields was inevitable. His strong addiction to drugs had put an end to the many hopes he had previously aroused. His life was in a constant decline, and he failed repeatedly. Nonetheless, he managed to retain his musical genius as a guitar player, and this saved him time after time. His amazing musical talent never left him, even in his worst moments.

* * *

The elderly woman, who seemed to be about 85 years old, was accompanied by a companion with a Far Eastern appearance. The two were in a group of American tourists who had stopped at the Alhambra complex for a visit to the magnificent Alcazaba castle. Suddenly the older woman, with her erect bearing and good hearing, heard sounds of music coming from a spot about twenty meters from the entrance to the castle. She noticed a guitarist surrounded by tourists. Her group proceeded towards the entrance to the castle, but the imposing woman signaled to her companion that she would like to approach the music and the surrounding group, even if this meant missing the visit to the famous castle.

The guide, who was acquainted with the old lady's whims, gave his consent, and in a minute or two the two were already among the group of tourists enjoying Steve's music. The guitar case with its considerable quantity of coins and several bills indicated that this had been quite a successful day. Steve was still playing 'Golden Earrings', the song that had attracted the old lady, when she and her companion joined the audience. She was glad that the music she knew so well continued for another three or four lovely minutes. The old lady stood and listened, extremely moved by Steve's music. Her presence on the bridge with her companion and her palpable excitement attracted the attention of some of the thirty or forty tourists who crowded around the musician. Steve mainly played popular tunes that had been written during the years 1930-1960 and that remained "evergreen", played and enjoyed repeatedly. Steve reached the end of the melody and the old lady surprised everyone by being the first to burst out in applause, unexpected from a woman her age. Nearly everyone else followed her example.

Steve began to play 'Green Fields', the well-known Spanish romance 'Forbidden Games', and also the touching melody 'Black Eyes' (known in

Russian as 'Ochi chyornye'). Each piece was drawn out, as though the musician had included encores in advance. Some single tourists were compelled to continue on their way, while others joined the audience.

And then something happened to change the atmosphere, initiated by the elderly woman, who was enthralled by the music and by the circumstances.

The old lady had a name, just like everyone else. Her maiden name was Angela Baker. Almost none of her acquaintances knew whether Angela was the name she had been called by her parents when she was born in Kansas City, Missouri, or whether it was a name she chose for herself when she first began to dedicate her life to helping others. This professional career of helping and devotion to others began at the age of 20 when she moved with her family to the city of Nashville, Tennessee. Her father was a pianist who made a living performing at family events and clubs, not a prominent musician in the musical city of Nashville. Angela fell in love with music thanks to her father and to the atmosphere in this city, considered 'the hometown of music'. She fell in love with the nursing career she had developed at a young age. Indeed, as her name indicated, Angela was an angel for the many patients she personally cared for or for whom she was responsible during her lengthy professional career as a hospital nurse. She even formed personal connections with many of the patients under her care.

Over the years she not only felt close to her patients but also became involved in a different type of relationship with the doctors. In three different periods of her life she combined her professional and romantic relationships with three senior doctors in three different hospitals where she worked in Nashville. Affairs with two of these doctors led to her dismissal from two of the hospitals. The reason was that the doctors were married. Both hospitals found it convenient and appropriate to silence the romantic scandals created by firing the outstanding nurse. The two betrayed wives demanded her removal in return for their cooperation in hushing up the affairs. So she was fired twice, Angela the professionally acclaimed nurse with the problematic personal life.

Each time, however, Angela was certain that her lengthy affairs would end in the divorce of the married doctor and in her own marriage. That was the impression she formed from the doctors' promises. Sometimes the promises given by the unfaithful doctors sounded sincere and sometimes less so. Angela's expectations endured for many years with no change in her personal status. The third and last discrete affair lasted three years (and was the shortest of the three). When the third affair ended she was not concerned of being fired as only she and the doctor knew about it. Since then, quite a few years had gone by in the life of the aging nurse, who retained her feminine and pretty looks despite her advanced age.

Then came a time when her dismal thoughts of missed marriage opportunities were suddenly suspended. It was five years after her last affair with the director of a reputable department at her current place of work. The change came about thanks to an affluent gentleman, one of Nashville's wealthy who was admitted to the cardiology department of the private hospital where Angela was working as a responsible and much appreciated nurse.

Denis Keaton had been admitted to her department three times, and each time he was given a private room, in fact a personal convalescence suite. The second and third times he was admitted, over the next two years, he asked, or rather declared that he would only come to this boutique hospital, Nashville Hug, if Angela would be his personal nurse. His demand was complied with, proving once again that 'money talks'.

He was not born Denis Keaton. His Romanian gypsy parents named him in keeping with their ethnic affiliation. He and his parents eventually found themselves in the United States. When they arrived in the promised land their son's name was changed from Imri Nuji to Denis Keaton. It was done in a roundabout way.

Denis Keaton was 63 when he was admitted to the hospital for the third time. Upon his release he felt that he had fallen in love with the 'angel' who took care of him so devotedly and lovingly. He sensed that he owed his recovery to her more than to the doctors, wonderful as they might be. Angela was very fond of him. She had mixed feelings the third time he was admitted to her department in two years. She was sorry to see that he was ill again, but she was also a little glad to see him. And here he was with her again. Denis was young in soul and spirit, with the creative energies necessary to become involved in an increasing number of business projects and to make the most of life's pleasures. His health problems had only a slight impact on these sensations and urges.

Two days before his release his heart had physically healed but he had become emotionally enamored with Angela, the head nurse. His feelings for her and his opinion of her urged him to invite Angela to the hospital's classy café, Great Pleasure. He planned that the next evening, when he was to be released from the hospital, he would tell her that he wished to invite her out in order to present her with a thank you gift for the three times he had been in the hospital, where she had cared for him so devotedly. He felt that he owed her his recovery. It was undoubtedly a good excuse to invite her to the café.

Angela was definitely excited. Since the conclusion of her discrete affair with the director of the reputable department years ago no man had aroused in her such feelings and she had come to terms with remaining an elderly (but certainly not 'aging', as she saw it) single much-appreciated nurse.

Her disappointments over the past years and her acceptance of them had left their mark in the form of a limited desire for romantic trysts. She felt in her heart that the encounter with Denis the next evening would be special. She was curious to see what he would give her. She suspected that Denis had asked Barbara, the wife of his business manager who visited him daily with her husband, to buy the gift. In any case, she was determined not to accept money. She wondered how the evening would develop. She had never met any of her many patients after work throughout her lengthy career.

The Great Pleasure café was as trendy as the cafés of New York, Paris, London, or any other busy city. It served as the venue for celebrations honoring the birth of babies, patient recoveries, and family events. The café resembled the lobby of a prestigious 5-star hotel. For the rich tycoons and political leaders of Tennessee it was the ultimate hospital, with its elegant café and bar.

The gift Denis presented to Angela was certainly unexpected. No one had to bring it to the hospital, not even Barbara, the manager's wife.

After three affairs with prominent married physicians, and several more short relationships, it suddenly happened in the most unexpected way. She received an incredible marriage proposal. He asked her candidly whether she would be willing to marry him the next week at city hall. At his death, she as his wife would inherit a large part of his considerable fortune and property amassed through hard work and ingenuity.

She noticed that he was wearing a conspicuous piece of jewelry. This particular type of jewelry was the topic of a song that her father liked to play at weddings. She herself loved the ballad, which told a charming gypsy legend. Denis had gypsy blood, although he seemed rooted in American culture. Angela immediately overcame her amazement, replaced by endless joy that surged through her when she heard his crazy marriage proposal. Denis's words reverberated within her: "Every day I felt my heart healing through its love for you…"

At the same time, she saw before her the symbolic piece of jewelry.

She quickly came to her senses. She had seen almost everything in life, what with patients, unfaithful doctors, hypocritical bosses, and subversive and critical colleagues.

Both sides posed conditions for marrying (even Denis, the proposer): Angela insisted that she continue working in her profession as head nurse until her retirement. Denis stated that of his fortune, worth over $30 million and bequeathed to Angela in the event of his death, ten percent would be given to his nephew in Brazil. He had once been very close to his nephew, although they had not been in touch for the past decade. But he would always have a warm spot for his nephew who for a lengthy period was the only target of his paternal feelings. Throughout those years Denis had distanced himself from his family and from society and became immersed in building up his fortune in a lumber business that operated throughout the southern US states. At a certain stage of his life and in strange circumstances, his contact with his beloved nephew was unexpectedly severed (a long story, which he never divulged, not even to Angela).

Angela and Denis were happily married for 19 years. They had no children but they enjoyed a wonderful relationship, the envy of any other couple their age and in their situation. They had a rich life, involving various types of social and voluntary activities; a life of culture and entertainment, sports and hobbies, and undying love.

When Angela's husband passed away she was 71 years old, six years past her retirement.

82 year old Denis remained conscious and lucid until the moment he died. On his deathbed in the magnificent villa in Nashville, in his last moments, he uttered two sentences to his beloved wife, caring for him at his bedside:

"Angelita my beloved, it was worth being hospitalized three times to earn your endless love."

And the second sentence before closing his eyes forever:

"When you die, many years from now, please leave your inheritance to whoever you w-i-s-h rather than to someone to whom you are obliged. And if possible, that person should remind you of our love. Thank you, the love of my life, the admirable wife of your gypsy man."

• • •

Fifteen years after Denis died, his widow Angela took a trip, realizing her dream to tour Europe and including in her itinerary places associated with the gypsies. On her diverse and fascinating journey she visited Romania, Hungary, Italy, France, and now Spain as well. Wherever she went she was occupied by the dramatic question: What would happen to the immense fortune she had inherited, worth $63 million (the $30 million at the time of her marriage had grown to $70 million, of which $7 million had been granted to the nephew in Brazil). Who would receive the major part of her inheritance? Neither she nor Denis had any children.

Angela donated $5 million to establish a new wing in her husband's memory at the Nashville Hug hospital where they had met.

She gave another $5 million to organizations supporting homeless gypsy families in Europe and the southern US.

She had not decided what to do with all the other millions remaining from the inheritance.

She was nearing her 86th birthday, an age when she would do well to give some serious thought to this important issue: To whom would she leave all the money and her vast fortune, after deducting a small percentage equaling several million dollars for Sue Sayun, her devoted Vietnamese companion?

"Could you please play the tune you were playing when I arrived, the one you played before 'Green Fields'?"

"'Golden Earrings' or 'Dark Eyes', ma'am?"

"'Golden Earrings'. Do you happen to remember the lyrics?"

"I think so, ma'am. From Peggy Lee's song, if I remember correctly. Would you like the lyrics, ma'am, before or after the music?"

"Before, please."

"There's a story the gypsies know is true,
That when your love wears golden earrings,
She (he) belongs to you.

An old love story that's known to very few,
But if you wear those golden earrings,
Love will come to you…"

Steve half recited and half sang the song a cappella in his hoarse voice.

Angela was extremely touched by the words, more than she had felt for the past 15 years since the death of her husband Denis. Steve reached the end of the first stanza he could remember and then replayed the song's enchanting melody.
Angela's group concluded their visit to the castle, and came to collect her and her genial Vietnamese companion, heading for the bus amidst the bountiful greenery.
In a moment the members of the group forgot their fascinating visit to the castle. They were all astounded to see Angela overcome by tears as the 'hippie with the guitar' continued to play the tune familiar to all members of the older generation. Almost all of them had known the song and its melody for decades.
For long moments after the music had ended Angela's tears continued to flow, filling the wrinkles on her face like the tiny rivulets that gushed through the channels under the bridge where Steve and his audience stood. Towards the end of the riveting tune Angela leaned on Sue the Vietnamese. At a certain note she opened her purse decisively and passionately and handed Steve a pile of bills held together by a rubber band. It was a thick wad. A quick glimpse showed a twenty dollar bill on top, and the total must have reached hundreds of dollars, if not more. Steve was astounded by her dramatic act and so were all the tourists, including those who had come with Angela, the 'strange lady'. Angela promptly gave Steve a note she had prepared with her telephone number and the number of her room at the hotel in Granada. She asked him tearfully to give her a call at 8 pm.

Steve did call her. In their short conversation she conveyed to him some essential information.

A week after Angela returned from Europe to Tennessee Steve came to her villa in Nashville to play the music she loved. He stayed at an apartment in Angela's spacious complex. Sue served him delicacies from the Vietnamese cuisine that she made for the lady of the house and for herself. He savored the delicious cooked meals.

Every day of music always included the tune he had played at Alhambra, as well as tunes she fondly remembered from her youth, gypsy tunes. In one of the most popular, 'Johnny is the boy for me', Angela replaced the name Johnny with Denis, and with Steve playing the guitar she joyfully hummed the alternate words to herself, 'Denis is the boy for me'.

In this song she always imagined the charming evening at the hospital café, where Denis Keaton proposed to her, pointing at his earring, and then admitted that he had brought the earring with him to the hospital, hid it and put it on before coming to meet her at the café, knowing as in the gypsy legend that Angela would be his wife. He recited the words of the song for her. In this way, the song always reminded her of their love. Of all the many renditions of the song 'Golden Earrings', Steve's was the most moving. On none of her CDs of the song and melody did she receive the same sense of joy as she did listening to Steve adeptly playing his guitar.

Three years after that incredible encounter at Alhambra, Adv. David Adams from the prestigious Nashville law firm of Adams & Adams summoned Steve William Bull to his office. After attending Angela's funeral Steve had found time to go and visit two childhood friends who had done well for themselves in San Francisco's Silicone Valley.

Steve flew back to Nashville and arrived at the law office on time for the meeting. Adv. David Adams read him Angela's will. The experienced lawyer, who had overseen many impressive last testimonies, was nonetheless amazed and found it hard to conceal his feelings. Angela had left Steve William Bull 95 percent of her property and money. She had also included in the will a short handwritten letter:

'Dear Steve, the man to whom I am not obliged to leave my inheritance, but the man to whom I certainly wish to leave my inheritance, with a clear and lucid mind... You are the man who always reminded me of my love, my boy with the golden earring, whom I loved so much. Thank you, Steve, and may you continue to bring joy to people everywhere with your wonderful sounds of life. And also remember that luck means: life, us, caring, karma.
We both had good karma and were lucky to meet caring people in our life. Enjoy your good luck and use it well... Good luck.
Yours,
Angela Baker Keaton'

Angela left the remaining five percent to her Vietnamese companion, Sue Sayun. She too had benefited from the four lucky letters, when Angela saw her working as a devoted maid at the fabulous Sofitel hotel in Hanoi, five years earlier. She brought her to Nashville to be her housekeeper and dedicated companion. Angela left a note in her will for Sue as well, with a shorter message:

'I love you, dear Sue. Now you are free to do as you wish and I hope you will soon find the man of your dreams. Yours with love and appreciation, Angela'

A year after Angela's death, millionaire Steve Baker (Bull) was running a large organization that helped young people overcome addictions to hard drugs using a musical therapy method that he himself had developed in memory of his days at Berkeley, to aid their rehabilitation.

The logo of the organization, which became quite prominent, featured a golden earring.
The theme song of the organization was Peggy Lee's same wonderful song, 'Golden Earrings', a song which has changed, and will go on changing, the lives of so many people…

It is never too late to fall in love,
it is never too late to become fortunate.

2

The mulatto, the artist, the dancer, and the mystic

● ● ●

At that point in time the Flamingo Dance Club with its endless reserve of beauty and sensuality, where Brazilian women danced to the rhythm of samba and lambada, was the best place for Dexter to spend his evenings and nights. Comprehensive blood tests recently performed in Houston, his Texas hometown in the US, had come back showing critical and tragic medical results. He had been diagnosed with a rare deadly blood disease. His personal doctor and another expert who had each separately examined the test results had given him the bad news. The doctors estimated that he had 6 to 8 months to live. Medication would add another 3-4 months to his life, but it would involve harsh side effects. Dexter, who was self-employed and addicted to his job, decided that the time had come to realize his fantasies involving the female sex, fantasies that had laid dormant for many years in the three phases of his life: before marrying Liza, during their marriage, and after the divorce. For the past five years he had not found time for a vacation outside his hometown.

Dexter, in his late forties, was naturally astounded at the bad news. He had indeed felt particularly tired from time to time in recent months, and also uncharacteristically weak. This sense of malaise had prompted his

GP to order the blood tests. He had not imagined that these would be the findings. A repeat test sadly confirmed the medical results.

Dexter's son and daughter knew that he had managed to survive two wars, fighting overseas in Iraq and Afghanistan as a lieutenant in the armed forces. His children understood that the current situation was much more serious. Their father was living on borrowed time.

His two good friends Ronald and Stan, who were familiar with Dexter's fantasies since his divorce, advised him to travel to Brazil in search of his dreams. They told him that the coastal city of Salvador welcomed veteran soldiers who were free to 'celebrate' as they wished. Dexter did not think twice.

Every day was significant. The cruel countdown had begun. He organized his affairs and packed a few clothes and personal belongings in a small suitcase, together with some books, including 'How to Change your Luck'. He was of course 'equipped' with his four specific fantasies. They were all associated with women. Dexter remembered that his parents had died at a young age, younger than he was now. On the flight to São Paulo and from there to Salvador de Bahia he was sorry that his hard working mother and father had been unable to take a similar 'death vacation', to prepare for the end of life while enjoying any pleasures they could.

Dexter was not particularly well-off financially, but he did okay and maintained a reasonable life style, and could even afford to fly to Brazil in the comfortable business class. He was able to spend some nice sums to reach his goals and to enjoy every moment of his limited time.

Four types of women had filled his thoughts and fantasies since deciding to travel to Salvador, in the state of Bahia, Brazil. He planned to find one of each type, allocating each a quarter of his time: a beautiful mulatto, a fascinating artist, a skilled samba dancer, and an attractive mystic. He would see how things developed. His anticipated encounters with the four unknown anonymous women reflected some of the loves of his life: diverse female beauty, the art of remote cultures, the joy of dance, and the spiritual metaphysical world. He felt that this was a fitting combination that would create a complete celebration. With his charm and his money, worth a lot in Brazil, he knew that he was capable of organizing the four parts of his 'pleasure trip' before reaching the end of his life. He was glad that he had foregone medication during the last three months, to avoid any harmful effects on his general, and particularly sexual, functions.

His long-term rental suite at the Viva Salvador hotel on the beach was extremely colorful, and he associated each color with a different element in his life.

Dexter spent six weeks, maybe the best in his life, at Salvador de Bahia. He felt that he couldn't have chosen a better way to treat himself before his impending death. This beautiful place offered all the pleasures of life in unlimited generosity, and all types of tempting and tempted women…

The four people dearest to him: his daughter Vera, his son Richard, and his devoted childhood friends Stan and Ronald, were at the Houston International Airport to welcome him home. They were all very worried. Two days previously he had called his two children from the hotel for the first time since leaving home. He had purposely severed all contact with the world, even with those closest to him, and left on a finite adventure taking no mobile phone.

After loving gestures and endless hugs, the two friends asked the son and daughter's permission to take their father aside and ask him one short question 'man to man'. They stood whispering for a minute or two. Dexter, who surprisingly looked very well and not sick at all, answered their question: "Yes, I fulfilled all my four fantasies and I will easily return to them again soon in Brazil …" His words sounded strange and vague, certainly considering his medical condition. At the same time, they couldn't wait for a more 'juicy' description. Their friend promised to 'fill them in' the next day, and to amaze them with a surprising story about his experiences. This only served to increase the mystery. He took his leave of Stan and Ronald.

His son and daughter took him home in the son's car. They told him that his physician had called a week ago asking for their father, but was unwilling to say why he was looking for him. "He only said that he wants to talk to you, dad". Richard the son had told the doctor that his sister Vera and himself were not in touch with their father in Brazil. The doctor found this hard to believe, he was completely astonished. Since then he had called the son three more times, but to no avail. No one knew Dexter's whereabouts. The doctor made the son promise that once his father returned he would ask him to call immediately, and said that he would be available 24 hours a day. And so it was. Dexter indeed made the call from the car, in the presence of his children, on the way home from the airport.

"Hello my friend, Dr. Isaac Samuel," said Dexter in a joyful voice that belied his diagnosed medical condition.

"Welcome, Dexter," said the excited and energetic doctor, not waiting for him to finish. He couldn't waste even a moment of the precious time. "On behalf of the medical center, the laboratories, and myself I ask for your deepest forgiveness: You are completely healthy!!! Sorry! Sorry! Sorry!" yelled the doctor in the voice of a radio announcer declaring the beginning of World War III, or describing the winning shot in the NBA basketball championship. Dexter, amazed, did not understand what was going on, and his reply froze on his lips. His two children were also in complete shock. The doctor remained focused and told his friend and patient that the next morning at 10 am he would await him at his clinic and tell him exactly what had happened. He suggested that his children should come too.

At 10 am Dr. Samuel greeted Dexter and his two children, Vera and Richard, with a hug, and said that he was extremely glad, so happy to be asking for his forgiveness and to apologize to him and his two children. "Twice the test results were replaced with those of someone else. There was a rare problem with the software… and your results, Dexter, are excellent, forget everything we told you… You have many more beautiful years to live".

His statements sounded like part of a televised drama series.

Dexter, shocked, hugged the doctor mightily: "I accept your apology with love and tears and thank you for the wonderful gift you have given me: Thanks to you I had the experience of a lifetime in Brazil. It would not have been possible if not for your positive tragic error. Better a critical mistake than a critical condition…"

Dexter's two devoted friends, Ronald and Stan, invited him to brunch immediately after the visit to the clinic and received two surprises… They needed time and energy to get over the shock…

Their friend told them of the inconceivable unbelievable medical error… and while they were still trying to get over the fantastic news he asked them: "And you must want to hear how I realized my four fantasies…"

Still in shock, they answered him together: the mulatto, the artist, the dancer, the mystic!

He replied, unfazed as usual: "Take a deep breath… during my entire visit to the wonderful city in Brazil... I was with one woman only... and I fell in love with her. Today I know that I will return to her in Salvador de Bahia, and that I have many more years to be with her...

When I am an old man, ninety years old, she, Fortuna, will be sixty. Until then we have another 41 years to live.

Not bad for someone who only two months ago had hardly one year left to live.

Which of the four is she: The pretty? The fascinating? The skilled? The attractive?"

Two weeks later, Dexter's two friends had fallen in love with Salvador de Bahia, its clubs, its streets full of dancing and carnivals, and its enchanting beaches...

But more than all, Ronald and Stan fell in love with the special woman called Fortuna... four women wrapped up in one... a beautiful mulatto, fascinating artist, exciting samba dancer, and attractive mystic. That is Fortuna...

Now they understood very well how Dexter's four fantasies could come true in one incredible woman...

'The wisdom of life is to enjoy what you have to the full, even when circumstances do not seem ideal'.

3

The blessing of the "three Ls" at the wedding in Varanasi

● ● ●

Dustin Harley woke up at 11 am in his room at the pleasant Star hotel in Varanasi, unable to decide whether last night's incredible experience was indeed real or part of a dream, causing him to sleep so late on his last day in India. In any case, even as a dream it was undoubtedly fantastic from beginning to end.

Upon awakening, the sentence that sprung to mind for the top-notch successful copyrighter from Sidney was 'Am I a butterfly who dreamt of being a man or a man who dreamt of being a butterfly?!' reflecting the blurring of dream and reality. It was hard for him to answer his own question. Dustin decided that he could not decide at the moment, and that in any case he was in no hurry. Breakfast at the hotel was already over and it was three hours before his personal guide to Varanasi would be coming to take him to the airport. It would have been impossible for him to leave the hotel and walk around on his own among the unruly crowds of believers who had come to participate in the sacred festival.

Lacking any alternative, he felt an urge to check out then and there whether last night's experience had indeed occurred or whether it was all part of a dream he had dreamt and that would disappear upon waking.

Dustin accessed the gallery of photographs and videos he had taken last night on his smartphone, to prove to himself that the fantastic story had indeed taken place. For confirmation, he searched for backup in the form of photographs on his state-of-the-art digital camera. These photographs as well proved, to his joy, that it was true… not another of the imaginary delusions so typical of his life.

The moment Dustin became convinced that yesterday's events had indeed happened and were not a trick of the mind, he received a telephone call that convinced him to prolong his stay in Varanasi for two more days, and to change hotels…

The entire wild incident had begun last night at 7:30 pm. Dustin was in his hotel room, talking on the phone to his girlfriend Audrey, at home in Sidney. He told her excitedly about his experiences the day before, on his second last day in India. He began with a description of waking up very early, at four am, when he was picked up by his personal guide and driver who took him to the steps of the main ghat on the Ganges. In that sacred river he was taken on a private boat with his guide and a rower, to watch the unique magnificent sight of the sunrise in all its stages and from every possible angle. He was astounded by the masses of half-naked worshippers in the river. From the boat he also observed the cremation ceremonies, popular among tourists. As he described it to Audrey, who hung on his every word, this had undoubtedly been a very tough experience, one that left him breathless and shaken.

Dustin had a poetic sensitive soul combined with significant skills of verbal expression, both written and oral. His personality and skills had been a major factor in his rapid promotion in less than two years, climbing the hierarchy of creative people within a flourishing global advertising firm.

His girlfriend, a successful fashion designer, had been fascinated over the past three weeks by his descriptions of his journey in India with Raji, the Indian guide appointed by the travel agent who had organized the wonderful trip. Dustin told her in detail about his day at the crowded festival in Varanasi. He described how he had to constantly hold on to the shirtsleeve of his dedicated guide, who made his way through the hundreds of thousands of celebrants. He went on to describe his visit to the nearby village of Sarnath, with its endless monuments commemorating Buddha in different postures and dimensions in this oft-toured town,

where the founder of Buddhism had given his first public sermon…
Suddenly Dustin paused and told his girlfriend that throughout their conversation, for the past fifteen minutes, he had been hearing live music from under the hotel. By its volume he estimated that it was coming from a large variety of musical instruments. "Maybe I'll be fortunate and have a chance to see a wedding procession; it's the only thing I haven't done on this perfect trip. I have not seen an Indian wedding. Maybe I'll have the karma to at least watch and attend the preliminary ceremony preceding the actual wedding…" he told his girlfriend excitedly and hastily.

Several times during his trip he had passed by wedding processions, but they had rapidly continued on their way.
He said goodbye to Audrey on the phone and hurriedly left his room, equipped with a camera in one hand and his smartphone in the other. Dustin sent out a message to the universe: 'I really want to be at an Indian wedding, I owe this to myself…' He had fantasized so often about experiencing an Indian wedding ceremony, if only the preliminary procession. He communicated this now, standing at the entrance to the hotel, encountering circles of joyful dancers within the impressive outer circle formed by the musicians. It was an authentic folklore spectacle. Once again he remembered that in geography lessons at school in Australia India had always been his favorite.

Suddenly he felt that the messages he was conveying to the cosmos from Varanasi, the sacred and sanctifying city, the enchanting and enchanted, must be taking root. On his last evening in India, at the last moment, he was at a wedding procession, with women dancing in special wedding saris, studded with expensive jewels and diamonds. Some fifteen musicians, most equipped with various types of wind instruments, began to play rousing music.

He photographed everything, gathering mementos of this exciting event from every possible angle.
He found himself chatting with two elegantly dressed men, some of the few wearing turbans. In answer to his question they told him that the wedding would be taking place shortly in the imposing wedding complex opposite the hotel. The complex was surrounded by impressive colorful lighting that increased his desire to personally witness the wedding ceremony. Among the many hundreds of Indian celebrants crowding into the courtyard outside the wedding complex were some dozen tourists

who were there by chance or had heard the commotion from their hotel rooms. Dustin was overjoyed at his luck on this magical trip, which was now complete. Only later on in this enthralling evening would he understand that the term 'complete' was premature, considering what was in store for him.

He had spent three magical and fascinating weeks, from the magnificent Sikh Golden Temple in Amritzar through holy Haridwar and Rishikesh with its Aarti ceremonies on the Ganges. From there he had continued to fascinating Delhi, and on to the Taj Mahal, one of the wonders of the world, in the city of Agra. Then on to Jaipur, capital of Rajasthan, the beautiful pink city with its elephants and castles. Then an incredible visit to Khajuraho with its dozens of temples full of hundreds of artistic creations featuring the erotic Kama Sutra positions. And finally, a visit to unique Varanasi… the only thing missing had been the Indian wedding. And now this event, even if only the preliminary procession, would complete the jigsaw puzzle of his 'ultimate experience' of India, as he had defined his trip to Audrey on the phone only one hour previously. But then the unexpected happened…

Suddenly a tall man wearing a gray suit and a blue tie, with a ponytail and thick-framed eyeglasses, appeared beside Dustin. Pleasantly, with a slight smile and soft voice, he greeted Dustin in English: "Good evening, sir". Dustin replied in kind. The stranger introduced himself as Viraj Brahasima Sing.
"It's a pleasure to meet you. I'm Dustin Harley from Sidney, Australia, and I'm fortunate tonight. This is my last evening in India, after three magical weeks, and I am finally realizing my dream to 'savor' an Indian wedding, or at least its first course".

He had no idea who the man was, what his words meant to the stranger, and where this encounter would take him…
"I am the father of the groom. We have come from Montreal, Canada, for the wedding of our eldest son Behlark with Bandura, a native of Varanasi. I'm glad that you're here among the guests celebrating before they reach the wedding complex."
"I am honored and excited to meet you, the father of the groom. I am so excited.." At that moment Dustin knew that the universe had heard his messages and wishes and sent him the groom's father. He felt that the cosmic being, or even the magical Indian karma, had given him a

wonderful opportunity not to be missed.

He grabbed onto that 'once in a life opportunity', used all his skills as a great copyrighter, and said to the groom's father: "Please give the young couple the blessing of the 'three Ls'..." Dustin made up a blessing on the spot, as though composing a slogan on the job in his advertising office in Sidney, a publicity slogan heading a major campaign. It was his special skill, the reason he had received this bonus trip to India from the management. He could have chosen any other destination in the world, but this country on the subcontinent had aroused his curiosity since childhood.

"And what is the blessing of the 'three Ls', if I may ask?" asked the groom's father politely, unable to restrain his curiosity.

"Love, Luck, Life," he listed promptly and naturally, as though this was a blessing he gave at least once a day. "The love of a wonderful relationship and abundant fertility... the luck of being in the right place at the right time with the right people... and a life full of the richness of joy..."

Viraj Brahasima, father of the impressive groom, could not believe his ears. All day long he had been trying to find a replacement for his brother, the professor, who was to have spoken at the wedding but had fallen sick that very morning. The groom's father had been looking for someone to speak in his stead. And here right before the opening of the gate to the complex, opposite the hotel, he had found a suitable candidate...

From here on everything happened, at least from Dustin's point of view, at a dreamy tempo and with wonderful karma that could only be his on this night. Since childhood he had been gifted with the ability to make things happen. Many of Viraj Brahasima's relatives and acquaintances could not understand how in these crucial moments before entering the magnificent wedding complex, the groom's father, a respected and esteemed person in his own right, remained 'engrossed', so they felt, for twenty precious minutes with a young man, a tourist unknown to any of them. None of them had any idea of the identity of the 'mysterious white man in jeans', as defined by the wedding guests attending the upscale glittering event, the majority of whom had come from the Indian diaspora in Britain and Canada and knew that their relative and acquaintance, Mr. Sing, was internationally renowned for his success. Although he was usually very easy to read, in these circumstances his disappearance from his dear relatives for several long minutes was definitely inexplicable, to say the least.

The magnificent gate of the wedding complex opened to the sound of many musical instruments, creating an atmosphere of a dramatic act preparing the guests for a special experience. Together with all the other guests, Dustin, the guest of honor of the groom's father, was dazzled by the fabulous wedding complex featuring dozens of specially designed food stalls offering tasty delicacies. Extravagant fireworks were lit at regular intervals, pyrotechnics combined with exquisitely illuminated water fountains; live Indian and Western music served as background, and segments of Bollywood films appeared on giant screens surrounding the incredible complex.

The bride and groom resembled a young royal couple, wearing crowns. They were posed above the crowd on a giant crane. Various acrobats entertained the many guests. A religious ceremony was held in the center of the garden, attended by the closest male relatives of the bride and groom, sitting Indian style on magnificent carpets. The ceremony was led by the groom's father and several holy men. Participants prayed and burned various objects in a bonfire, trilling wedding tunes.

The guest of honor, invited to sit beside the groom's father with the closest relatives and holy people, was none other than Dustin Harley, who only a short while earlier had sent out his plea-wish to the universe. Here he was, realizing his dream to personally experience an Indian wedding in full force, at a magnificent event by any standard. At this wedding he was not only a guest, one of the many thousands attending the event, and not only a guest of honor, but the 'star of the evening'… At the urging of the most important person at the wedding, everyone was seeking Dustin's proximity and attempting to make his presence and time as enjoyable as possible, honoring him in the spirit of the generous event. The waiters catered to his every need and constantly offered him delicacies and colorful cocktails. The most prominent relatives attempted to remain in his vicinity. They told him about the family and praised the impressive deeds and admirable personality of Viraj Brahasima Sing, the groom's father, who had extended his business from Mumbai to Montreal. Dustin felt adrift in an enchanted world. He suddenly felt like Harry Potter who finds himself at a wedding in Varanasi, the most sacred Hindu city. In the company of the groom's father, the wedding seemed to him like a magical event. A skilled copyrighter, he was unable to find a fitting superlative for this moving and uplifting situation.

Only two hours ago the groom's father had first seen him outside the wedding complex and invited him to be his guest of honor and to give his blessing to the newlyweds, thanks to the 'LLL' he had thought up on the spot.

The giant festive crane brought the couple down on a couch placed in the center of the stage facing the glittering well-dressed guests, impressive quantities of diamonds and precious jewels embedded in the women's dresses and adorning their bodies.

Inconceivably, at the beginning of the wedding ceremony Dustin was invited to ascend the stage and sit by the bride, while the groom's father sat next to his son on the other side of the couch. In these unbelievable moments he imagined that if his physician parents and his girlfriend Audrey would have happened across the wedding and seen him in the present situation, they would probably have fainted and required medical attention.

Several sentences were uttered in Hindu by a holy man who joined them, standing behind the couch with the couple and the groom's father. At that moment Dustin was certain that his beating heart could be heard on the other side of the complex. The sound of his heart beating probably equaled that of the drums that had been beating all evening, from the preliminary procession to the present…

"I have the pleasure and the honor of inviting my good friend, Mr. Dustin Harley, a guest of honor who came all the way from distant Australia to the wedding of our dear son Behlark and our dear daughter Bandura, and whom I have asked to bless the happy couple on behalf of us all…"
It was obvious to anyone acquainted with Viraj Brahasima Sing that his presentation of the foreigner from Australia carried the marks of a Bollywood drama. The use of such a dramatic cinematic element was not surprising in the case of Mr. Sing, a successful Bollywood producer who had recently opened a studio in Montreal as well.

The young man with the jeans and sports blazer, wearing a t-shirt and sneakers, a foreigner who had added a sense of mystery to the event, now posed an even bigger riddle for many of the guests, who could not understand how he had won the honor of blessing the couple. Many continued to wonder about his identity and what he was doing here on the central stage at the wedding. Why and how had he become so close to the esteemed Bollywood producer? Maybe he was a western film star, Canadian or otherwise, who was not well known here in India. Mr. Sing had been telling his acquaintances that he, with his Bollywood film productions, strives to conquer America... The wedding had turned into a mysterious drama, a mysterious karma...

The young Australian concluded his 'three Ls' blessing, which as a copyrighter he had managed to develop and expand into an entire speech, since inventing it for the groom's father three or four hours earlier, a short while that seemed like an eternity. The audience thanked him by waving and applauding loudly. Descending from the stage he was greeted with bows, handshakes, and warm slaps on the back.

In these euphoric moments he felt that he was descending from the stage at the premier of his own movie. For several seconds he thought of the advertising office where he worked, and where he wished he would be promoted from composing texts, slogans, radio ads, internet posts and banners, to ad writing. He hoped that from there it would then not take him long to become a screenwriter. That had been his longtime dream.

In his speech on stage he had spoken of the first 'L', love, and linked it to the human heart, with its two ventricles. "Neither can exist without the other, as in love. It is the fuel that stimulates lovers and connects them to each other..." The audience, most of whom spoke English, welcomed his words.
Then he spoke of the second 'L', luck. He suggested that the couple follow his example and always do their best to be in the right place at the right time, as he had been this evening with Viraj Brahasima Sing. He did not mention that their meeting had been completely random as he did not want to solve the riddle of their relationship, rather to leave it in its mysterious form at least until the end of the evening.

After speaking at length about the elephant as an Indian symbol of luck and blessing them with lots of luck, he continued to the third 'L' of the evening, life. He wished them that their life would be full of content, giving, and fulfillment of all their dreams.

He said that "nothing gives one strength like giving of oneself". He concluded with warm heartfelt thanks to Mr. Sing and to the happy couple and their entire family. He said, "You have given me the best gift from beautiful India, and this evening I have tried to give you a small gift of my own in my blessings to you…"

The heartfelt applause at the conclusion of his speech, together with the tears of the groom and bride, left Mr. Viraj Brahasima Sing, the successful producer of Bollywood films in Mumbai and Montreal, in no doubt as to his business proposal to Dustin Harley at the end of the evening.

The next morning Viraj Brahasima Sing paid the Australian airline a significant sum to postpone Dustin's return flight to Sidney by two days, while also upgrading him to business class, all through his office manager in Mumbai.

Both people involved in the signing of Dustin Harley's employment contract as a senior screenwriter for Mumon Film in the high-class hotel in Varanasi two days later were very pleased and excited, and the firm's lawyer, who had also attended the wedding two days earlier, proposed a toast.
Incidentally, Dustin the copyrighter immediately figured out the significance of the name Mumon, a combination of the first syllables of Mumbai and Montreal. In his work he always searched for links between words, and in his life he looked for links with the right people. The signing ceremony that day was the best proof that he was adept at detecting both word links and people links.

Over two years after that unbelievable wedding night in Varanasi, this was the state of affairs in our cosmic world, and in the life of the main characters:

Dustin and Audrey Harley were living happily and quite comfortably in Montreal, with occasional trips to Mumbai, he as the senior screenwriter of Mumon Film and she as the main costume designer for the company's film productions. They were expecting their first baby, a boy, in a month's time.

The producer, Viraj Brahasima Sing, had expanded the marketing of his company's films to the West, with considerable success in Canada, Australia, and the United States.
A major factor in this success was a movie that had attracted many

millions of viewers in India and the West, "LLL: A life of luck and love in Varanasi", by screenwriter and director Dustin Harley and producer V.B. Sing, of the multinational Indian Mumon Film company.

One moment can change your entire life. It is important to do everything to create such a moment. It is certainly worth a try!

4

"Monokini"
at Croatia's islands

• • •

That summer Bobitz Beach in the Dalmatian islands, opposite the shores of Croatia, was teeming with students from all over the country who had come for a vacation at the enchanting location. They had come in search of a good time on the beautiful beaches of the magnificent islands, some of which were known for their nudist enclaves. Hundreds of young people studying at the universities and colleges of Croatian Dubrovnik and Split had all headed for the Bobitz Beach club on one of the islands. The place had developed a reputation for offering students and other young people a chance of some carefree and liberal fun. There were lots of parties, original productions, sing-along evenings, fashion shows, food and jewelry fairs, and above all, personal encounters and dating events. The organizers and producers of this considerable enterprise demonstrated original and creative thinking on the dating scene, which was the main attraction. Events included prize-winning games and quizzes, all under the innovative title "fate date".

Beginning from the second of the four days everyone was excitedly preparing for the final competition. No one knew what it would include, but the prizes were disclosed to the vacationers in advance. The young lady who would win first prize could choose any man she wished to spend the night with her, and the reverse would be true of the winning man, who could choose any woman. At this stage, in order to arouse interest in the competition, the organizers said that everyone taking part had to accept the rules whereby he/she could be chosen by the winner for the night, with no refusals.

In almost every group there are those designated 'most popular'. This is true of schools, youth movements, the military, colleges, parties, singles events, and even events for… the elderly.

Here too, among the many Croatian students who had come to relax and mainly to have a good time and get to know each other, there was one young lady who was the sensual and attractive 'star', a third-year student at a well-known college of design. She herself was a combination of beauty and sensuality, joie de vivre and self confidence, a cross between a young lady and a mature woman. Her name was Anna Kostitz. She clearly enjoyed the attention she attracted among the opposite sex. And this happened everywhere and at all times: by the bar, at the hotel pool, at beach parties, at various social events, and in restaurants as well. Many students tried to attract her attention, as well as her heart… but two days had gone by and she was still unattached. At least that's how it seemed. She was an attractive target, but she remained a guarded fortress. Meanwhile no one had found the way to her heart.

26 year old Zelico Dardovitz was one of those students not known for their handsome appearance. He was also not successful with the female sex. However he was extremely knowledgeable. He was studying agricultural economics at a much respected academic institution. His close friends attested to his 'wasted romantic soul'. For him, as for many others, this vacation was an opportunity to meet a large number of women in a relatively short time and to take a break from the intensive routine of studies and permanent or temporary jobs. Every evening, Zelico waited for the quizzes and social competitions to demonstrate his inner qualities and 'compensate' for his less than impressive physical appearance.

The organizers of the vacation, a company called Sensuous Creativity, spared no original and daring idea to stimulate and excite the participating students.

The winners of the final competition could take their pick of all those present for one night of pleasure.

Zelico knew that this was his opportunity to win the favors of Anna, at least for one night. This would give him a chance to persuade her of his virtues, although self confidence was definitely not his strong point.

The topic of the final competition was kept a complete secret until the very last moment. It was only known to the director of the company, his assistant, and the moderator of the competitions.

Over 300 students, a record number, attended this final event.

The moderator, Dushko, announced: "The winners of this evening's competition will be offered the company of the most attractive male and female students. The topic is: Something creative associated with the... sea. Competitors are requested to compose a short story, write an original poem, present a dramatic scene, create a drawing, take a photograph, or produce any concise work of art associated with the sea. Those chosen to participate will have 30 minutes and everyone else will be the judges. After all the ideas and artwork are presented, the male and female winners will be determined by vote".

The first 10 women and 10 men to raise their hands were chosen by the moderator to take part in the competition. In the thirty minutes they had to create their ideas and artwork everyone else danced, chatted, laughed, and kept busy meeting other people and having conversations over a glass of wine, beer, or a cocktail. Everyone was eager to see what the twenty contestants had prepared.

The high quality productions would not have put any Croatian 'Idol' show to shame.

Chubby Nula, a math and accounting student with a prominent scar on her forehead, easily came in first with her beautiful sketch of students sailing on boats that turned into bars on the sea. The title of her piece was: "A Sea of Bars on the Sea". She chose a night with Ivan, an attractive male student. Nula gave Ivan her impressive sketch, and in return he gave her himself (all, part, or some) for the night, as determined by the rules of the competition.

It was one of Zelico's happiest evenings. His artwork won most of the applause of the judging audience. He chose as his prize to spend the rest of the night with Anna. Zelico dedicated his artwork to Anna. She hugged him when he gave her the poem he had written, entitled 'Monokini'. The more discerning noticed the slightly lascivious sly wink aimed at Anna by the moderator Dushko.

These were the words and rhymes read by the winner, a graduate student:

Monokini

'It began on its own
On a warm summer day
When we read in the paper
And did not know what to say.

Concerned fashion manufacturers
Were selling less clothes
Women had stopped wearing
Bathing suits in droves.

And less means
That more was exposed
Of their upper parts
As they proudly posed

And the bottom,
What a shame…
It alone remained covered
By a fabric of fame…

The waves boiled and roiled
Refusing to see
How half a bikini was lost
To the female sex in the sea

And the minimal costume became
A matter of current affairs
And raised the blood pressure
Of beachgoers everywhere

And the name suggested
For a garment so teeny
Was not a g-string
But rather… monokini'

Anna Kostitz was quite admirable when the competition ended at midnight and she found herself on the beach with Zelico, where he once again read her his poem 'Monokini', the poem that was now hers and that had earned him the privilege of being with her. They sat till morning and told each other about themselves and about life in general. She enjoyed talking to him. He was shy. The night brought with it no further intimacy, aside from two light hugs, laughing about last night's game. They were strongly illuminated by the full moon but it did not create a romantic atmosphere.

At four am they separated. 'Anna the beautiful', as Zelico called her that night, thanked him profusely for his poem, personally dedicated to her. She promised him to make good use of it.

He walked her back to her hotel room. Before they separated she told him that he is a pleasant, intelligent, and high-class guy, but that he lacks self confidence. In return for the poem she said that she would like to give him something that she had written in the past and that was always with her. She took a notebook from her purse and wrote down the words on a piece of paper, which she then handed to him. She asked him to read these few words only after he returned from his vacation in the Dalmatian islands. And he complied with her request.

* * *

Nine years passed and life brought Dr. Zelico Dardovitz and Anna Kostitz-Ivkovitz together in far different circumstances. She was now 32 years old, and he was three years older.

They had been invited to Dubrovnik to speak to recent university graduates. The title of the session at which they had been invited to lecture was 'Fortuitous successes'.

They were invited by Dushko Ivkovitz, the former moderator, who had since become a popular moderator at events and conventions. He located Zelico fairly easily through Google. Finding Anna Kostitz was even easier.

Dr. Zelico Dardovitz, a popular expert in marine agricultural economics in developed countries, was happy to come. His romantic soul found it nostalgic, reminding him of his days as a (graduate) student.

Two days at a reputable hotel in Dubrovnik with his wife in return for the lecture also seemed to him a tempting offer. The timing was right as he had just returned from a grueling professional trip to Central America. He remembered Dushko, the comic moderator from the vacation that had had such a profound effect on his self-confidence. Dushko also told him that Anna Kostitz, the 'star' of that vacation in the Dalmatian islands, had also been invited to lecture, as she was now a successful business woman. Despite being married and a father and in such different circumstances, the successful agricultural economist felt his interest aroused. 'I wonder what happened to her after that moonlit night?' he thought to himself. His wife Melina, a recently licensed physician, had heard his story of 'Anna the beautiful' and the 'Monokini'. She loved the story, and she was glad that he had told it to her before they were married.

Anna, who had won acclaim in the media over the past two years as a successful career and business woman, was the first to speak to the new graduates beginning their professional life. The grand convention hall at the magnificent hotel was bursting at the seams. The moderator Dushko introduced Anna to the audience of university graduates.

She began by describing how, when still a student of design, a poem called 'Monokini' had been dedicated to her at a student vacation on the Dalmatian islands. She could still recite it by heart. Anna said that the poem, bestowed on her by an insecure graduate student, had had a great effect on her life. It won a competition and was dedicated to her, and then inspired her to design Monokini bathing suits. This was after she completed her fashion design studies, and for several years she has been successfully importing the garments to Europe, under the brand name 'Annakini'. Inspired by this enterprise she became a popular business woman and an advocate of women's liberal rights. She paused in the description of her career and recited 'Monokini' from memory:

'It began on its own…' she recited in full as if this was a play and she the main character… Reaching the end of her recital she continued to present her insights on success in business in particular and in life in general.

The applause was loud and enthusiastic and continued for some time.

At its conclusion the moderator invited Dr. Zelico Dardovitz to speak. The doctor had not heard Anna's lecture, he had been behind the scenes at the time. He began by relating that nine years ago he had had a non-romantic encounter with a wonderful woman. "When we separated she gave me a note in her handwriting that changed my life. I have kept the note ever since, and I will now read it to you… maybe it will change your life too…"

Anna looked at Zelico. She was astounded; she could not believe it… The note she had given him had changed his life, and here he was, Dr. Dardovitz, now a worldwide success, thanks to her…

Zelico took the note out of his shirt pocket, winked at Anna, and read in his tenor voice, stressing each and every word:

'Have faith in your abilities
Trust trust your way
Believe believe believe in your strength
And say amen amen amen'

The audience was amazed at the two stories, his and Anna's. It was hard to decide which of the two was the most incredible.

The moderator Dushko asked and was given a turn at the imposing lectern. He told the audience that "the woman who changed Dr. Zelico Dardovitz's life, when he was a student, is no other than the previous speaker, Anna Kostitz, world leading Monokini designer and manufacturer, popular women's rights advocate... The prominent doctor you see on stage received the note he just read to you from Anna when he presented her with 'Monokini', the poem he had written for her and dedicated to her..."
"Would you like to tell us about your enterprise, Dr. Zelico Dardovitz?!"
"Of course. This note remained in my wallet since I received it from 'Wonder Anna', and with my faith, trust, and belief I completed my doctoral studies and gave myself a wonderful opportunity to establish guidance centers for marine agriculture in the Americas. There, together with my team, I train local residents to realize their full personal potential and to believe in their own capabilities. A prestigious UN organization joined our enterprise several years ago. I owe much of this to the note that became my guide in life and helped me change from an insecure young man to one who makes the best of his abilities..."
The silence in the hall was absolute. Everyone was fascinated and astonished by the incredible unexpected discoveries that followed each other...
"Each and every one", continued Dr. Zelico Dardovitz, "has abilities and potential waiting to be realized and utilized... With Anna's permission I would like to devote the content of this note to everyone present...
'Have faith in your abilities, trust your way, and let me add, believe in your personality. And say amen amen amen!'

The moderator related that he had located Zelico after an interval of nine years and brought him and Anna together this evening, here on stage, nine years after they had first met at the students' event at the Bobitz

Beach club, previously described by Anna.
The audience reached new heights of amazement, but then they became even more incredulous…

After a minute's pause, which seemed to last forever, the moderator Dushko went on to say that… "My beloved wife Anna Kostitz has asked me to reveal the following information to Dr. Zelico Dardovitz, Kroatia's young star, with his self confidence and belief in his abilities…"
Now it was Dr. Zelico Dardovitz's turn to hold his breath, before the affable moderator continued: "As early as the first evening of the event at the Dalmatian islands I, as moderator, found a way of secretly 'hitting on' Anna. No one appeared to have noticed. She responded in confidence. We kept our romance a secret and managed to hide it from everyone. We secretly met at night on the beach. We sent each other lots of romantic SMS messages. As a moderator I wanted to retain the image of a professional who does not mix romance with my job as leader of the event, so we did everything to keep our relationship discrete…", he took a sip of water and continued his fascinating revelation:
"Beautiful Anna, however, wanted to enjoy her status as a single 'princess'. On our first night together I gave her a note with a few lines about self-faith. Wishing to help Zelico the insecure student, she gave him a slip of paper with the words she had received from me, and these proceeded to change his life. She said that she had written them down to increase their significance for him and this is what happened… all for the best."

The level of amazement in the hall rose yet again, with Dr. Zelico Dardovitz probably the most amazed.

Dushko 'the compelling moderator' paused and asked astonished Zelico to "recover and continue".

Dr. Zelico Dardovitz decided to cooperate with the series of confessions and to raise the level of amazement among those present to new heights… he winked at the moderator and at Anna, and invited her to come stand by him while he spoke…

"To tell you the truth, it was not me who wrote the winning poem, 'Monokini', rather I received it from a friend of mine. He was not with us on that mystical vacation to the enchanting islands. My friend, whose name I can't disclose, had copied my answers on a major test, and as a mark of his appreciation he gave me 'Monokini', a cute poem that he wrote in class when we happened to be together. This friend left the field of agricultural economics and achieved success in creative aspects of the local media…"

The audience was in shock. None of those present would forget this encounter for a long time. The three people on stage, Anna, her husband Dushko, and Zelico (whose wife was in the audience) were very excited.

Dushko the moderator concluded the session, thanked his beloved wife Anna and the successful fascinating economist and said: "Dr. Zelico Dardovitz, you have set the tone this evening… we owe you… and before we all go our way", he said to the audience: "Once again you have seen proof that 'All the world's a stage, and all the men and women merely players'… thank you and good luck!"

'Have faith in your ability, believe in your way, trust your deeds, and say Amen to success, which is sure to come your way!'

5

Sculpted avocado pits

● ● ●

It had been a tough year for avocado growers in a central African country. The demand from Europe, the main export market for their product, was lower than anticipated. They had held an extensive marketing campaign in various countries but it had not been as successful as expected. A large quantity of the fruit had been flown mainly to the British Isles, France, Germany, and Scandinavia, but orders were disappointing. As a result, the price of avocado in wholesale markets and retail sales points dropped that year.

In light of the circumstances, the growers' association Avocadia, encompassing a major part of local orchard owners, decided to hold a contest in Europe for creative ways of promoting the fruit. The first prize offered, a sum of 150,000 euros, was of course very attractive. There were also 200 secondary prizes of safari holidays in Africa for two. Avocadia was inundated by a flood of ideas, sent by e-mail to the contest website launched by the organization. There were over 450 different suggestions for food recipes. Well-designed booklets and catalogues were also received, offering a variety of recipes. Over 140 different suggestions for avocado-based beauty and skincare preparations arrived. Creative thinking generated other ideas as well, such as opening a chain of avocado-based restaurants, with or without supplements, serving salads, spreads, soups, pies, quiches, sandwiches, and even desserts such as surprising ice creams made of this special fruit. The contest also attracted recipes for avocado drinks, with or without alcohol.

Professional publicists sent digital posters sporting slogans. There were even 15 prescriptions for 'folk remedies' for curing various illnesses and solving physiological problems using the skin of the avocado and/or its meat. Submitters claimed that the curative qualities of the fruit had been proven.

A total of 2,300 people from all over the continent took part in the competition. They all consented on the participation form to any use of their ideas even if these do not win the contest. It was a basic condition of participation.

The first prize was split between three different participants who suggested the exact same idea, and each received 50,000 euros.

The first was a single architect from Bergen, Norway, by the name of Lars Johanssen. He made good use of his victory and became a popular interviewee on national media, a celebrity. Many women wished to make his acquaintance and in a short while he married a beautiful woman from Oslo (one of the many beauties of this city).

The second, Rita Jurgens, a teacher from Hamburg, received a tempting offer following her success, and proceeded to establish a creative pedagogical center for local youth. The proposal for this initiative was put forth by a foundation invested in teen education. In time she was asked to repeat her success in four other cities in northern Germany, becoming a 'guru' of innovative thinking in her country.

But the real story was that of the third winner, Jerry Cummings, a young unemployed man from Leeds, England. Previously, he had not been very lucky. For over a year he was an unemployed engineer and had quite despaired of finding a job. During this time his fiancé left him in favor of his good friend. And most unfortunate, he had contracted a chronic illness that affected the digestive system and for which no cure had been found. Then an ad on the internet attracted his attention, posted on the website of a manpower firm. The ad promoted a quick weeklong course entitled 'How to turn lemons into lemonade'.

Jerry did not hesitate and spent 250 pounds from his savings to join the course. He felt that this time something good would happen to him. Stephanie the instructor, a typically smart and temperamental redhead, had the complete attention of Jerry and the 30 other participants. In her teaching, she demonstrated how to turn a problem into an opportunity, a disadvantage into an advantage, and how to find the good in any bad. She brought many diverse examples illustrating how to implement such creative and positive attitudes. Of them all, one in particular remained in Jerry's mind.

It was the authentic story of a student who had searched for a job one summer in her US hometown but was rejected despite over 20 interviews. So she decided to stop going to interviews. Despairing of her job search she convinced herself that something good would come of her failures. The student remained at home and wrote a book based on her bitter experience, named: 'How to search for a job, and why I didn't find it'. She described and analyzed every mistake and error she had made in each job interview.

At the conclusion of a prime time interview on a national television channel, after her book reached the top of the best seller list, she said: 'Thank God I didn't find a job'.

A week after the intensive and informative course in Leeds, Jerry saw the online ad for the avocado promotion competition.

He wracked his mind, using methods he had learned from Stephanie the redhead, and of course asked himself what was the worst thing about avocado that could help promote the fruit. He thought and thought… and suddenly it came to him… He said to himself: the avocado pit, which constitutes a major part of the fruit, is discarded but raises the price considerably. Jerry promptly thought: 'So what is so good about that bad feature?…'

And from this conundrum he arrived at the idea that he then proposed to Avocadia, which just happened to be the same one sent in by the Norwegian architect and the German teacher.

All three, from such different places and backgrounds, had the same idea: to hold a competition for carving and sculpting avocado pits. The judges unanimously awarded the first prize to the three.

The idea was rapidly implemented and in each country where the fruit was marketed by Avocadia a separate competition was held, where avocado pits were transformed into artwork. Many people all over Europe went to work on the fruit. In a creative rapture they extracted the pit and hurried to take part in the various carving competitions. Many of them bought the fruit for the first time in their life. The next season saw a surge in the demand for avocado in Europe.

The directors of Avocadia became fond of Jerry. They appointed him a judge in the final artwork competition held in Dublin, Ireland, at the beginning of the next season.

By the time the competition came around he was completely healthy, cured of his hereditary disease. It happened like this: After he won the prize he asked the director of Avocadia, whom he had befriended, if some of the participants had also sent in ideas for avocado cures. The director replied in the affirmative and showed him all 15 ideas for 'folk remedies'. Jerry surveyed them all (as the participants had given their consent to publicize the ideas submitted). One of these attracted Jerry's attention in particular. It was a prescription referring specifically to his disease. He contacted the person who had submitted the idea, Irina, a Frenchwoman of Armenian descent who lived in Lille. She told him that this illness had been common in her family, with its origins in the Armenian part of Russia, for the past three generations. When her extended family arrived in France they discovered the curative qualities of the avocado. Her grandmother, who was an expert in folk medicines, cooked the fruit with three other ingredients. As a result, all family members were completely cured of the illness. Rumors of the wonder reached other patients in the vicinity, who somehow managed to obtain the 'miraculous avocado cure' and recovered from their illness.

Jerry Cummings flew to Lille. In six weeks the folk remedy managed to cure him completely.

He decided to share the prize with Irina the Frenchwoman. Together they opened a factory for manufacturing the medicine, named Avoca-mama. They marketed the miraculous cure to thousands of European patients on their website. The large majority were cured. The medicine jar carried a photograph of Irina's Armenian grandmother.
Irina soon became a successful business entrepreneur. Inspired by Jerry, she established a flourishing business employing some dozen Armenian women from her family. They designed beautiful artwork from avocado pits and marketed them successfully in France on the internet.
At the same time, elderly Armenian women who lived in her area introduced her to 'alternative folk cures' and these too were marketed online...

Jerry became a popular lecturer in Europe and the United States. He lectured on 'Avocado: the victory of creativity', became a world 'guru' on the subject, and was compensated accordingly.

Irina travelled from city to city throughout Europe with a mobile exhibit of avocado carvings.

Irina's daughter, Sabin, managed the online marketing of the folk remedies.

Jerry waived his part in the royalties received from his cooperative enterprise with Irina. His cure was worth everything for him. His former fiancé wanted to renew their relationship but he was happy with Adriana, Irina's cousin, whom he had met in Lille, France. A rich menu was planned for the forthcoming wedding of the loving couple, with avocado playing a main part in both the culinary and design art.

Avocadia shares are currently marketed on the stock exchange and their value is constantly on the rise...

'Even what seems like refuse can support you until a ripe old age...'

6

Enlightenment in the desert

• • •

Eileen, the director of a production company, entered the room with its ugly linoleum floor, neon overhead lighting, and dismal white walls, on the second floor of a building of small offices. She had no idea what a profound effect the place and the people she would meet there were to have on her life.

Eileen was in her fifties, having recently experienced a deep and painful crisis in her marriage. She had come in the hope of finding a way of uplifting herself and restarting her crumbling life.

Eight people sat facing the door, men and women of all ages, from young people to women her own age. The transition began once she took one of the empty seats and saw the man who was to guide the workshop this coming year. Her face lit up... You know that moment when you see smiling eyes, a radiant face, and understand that you have arrived? That this is the right place for you? This was such a moment for Eileen.

Three more people joined and the session began with an introductory round. There was an embarrassing moment when everyone glanced to their left and right, Jeremy the moderator smiling his charming smile and looking around. Aware of her difficulty remembering names, Eileen had adopted a technique. She proceeded to identify each person in the room with the first image that they aroused in her mind. One was a lion, another a wasp, the third a rabbit, and other such strange images, intelligible only to her. In time she was astonished at her strong intuitions in matching people to their images.

The workshop was planned to last an entire year, once a week for three hours a session. After Jeremy's introduction in the first session, Eileen eagerly awaited the next. She had many good qualities, but she was also impatient. She found it hard to accept things as they are and wanted more and more, and most importantly 'as quickly as possible'. So her family was very surprised that she was willing to commit to an entire year. They didn't realize what she had understood when first seeing Jeremy – that this place, these sessions, would change her life.

The sessions were accompanied by moments of strong emotions, alternating with tears and happiness, while understanding the potential for forgiveness, and what this forgiveness could do for her life. They also involved breaking conventions and constructing new ones. Eileen progressed hand in hand with the other members of the group, who had ceased to be strangers and had become a type of intimate family. With Jeremy's help, they reached a place that was less painful, more forgiving, more accepting and understanding, where the trauma they had experienced in their personal lives could result in new growth.

Eileen, a beautiful but reserved woman, could not believe the states of anger, rejection, misunderstanding, and fortification that she allowed herself to experience. At some moments she would ask herself: 'Why do I need this, this mental exposure, this emotional baring?! It leads me to breakdowns, to such hurtful places…' But she did not give up, and each time she left the room with the neon and the linoleum she found that she had climbed another rung on the difficult ladder of her choice.

One day Jeremy threw a 'bombshell'. He announced that he was travelling abroad for a month and someone else would be replacing him as moderator of the workshop. He asked how the group felt about this development.

Eileen fiercely objected. She said to Jeremy defiantly: "I am finally climbing the ladder and managing to breathe. How can I possibly go on without you?!"

Jeremy smiled his winning smile and said: "Eileen my dear, there is a time for everything. This must be the right time for you to change your life".

She came to the next session with a sense of strong resistance to the new moderator, Lia. She felt uncomfortable about her feelings of antagonism, as Lia was a charming, kind woman, completely devoted to the group. She always wore white, a real fairy godmother. Slowly all objection dissipated.
Eileen decided to embrace Jeremy's maxim that 'This must be the right time…'

After three sessions Lia suggested that they meet at a remote location to which they would travel together, a change of atmosphere… in the desert, for two days of observation. Eileen was glad for the suggestion; she understood that any change would help her in her quest.

The session in the Grand Canyon desert, in the state of Arizona, was very stimulating and different. This was where Eileen first began to feel a woman. Something about the silence in the desert helped her realize her femininity, grasp that the change was not only internal but external as well, that her constant rejection of anything 'feminine', of female friendships, might not be right for her at this stage in life. She sat in the desert facing the sunset, spread her arms, closed her eyes, and feeling attuned to herself said to the Godly presence: "I'm in your hands, I let go of my anger, my strong hold on my 'self', and open myself to a new and softer place in life". Although the wind was blowing it was a moment of silence; silence of the soul and silence of the desert. The Godly presence was there.

It was a moonlit night. Eileen was completely focused on herself, on a sense of understanding and misunderstanding, a sense that something bigger than her was happening, something that she can't understand, a type of mysterious circle that affects each and every individual in the world. She entered the Indian teepee, approached the bed that had been allocated to her.

It was a cold night in the canyon desert. She took stones from the desert, put them on the radiator near her mattress to heat them and placed them under her bed. She arranged the sheet on the mattress and suddenly felt something underneath. Eileen pulled it out and saw that it was a small leather satchel. She opened the satchel and found a note with a short love poem… she felt that maybe it was not meant for her eyes, but could not stop looking at the words that had so touched her soul. These were words that she had always hoped to hear from a man who loved her, words of unending, authentic love, from the bottom of the heart, with no 'give and take'; pure love, that probably does not exist, maybe only in poetry. It was written in a clear handwriting. Eileen felt that the words had been penned in longing for a beloved woman, a woman who would be part of the writer's life. She read the words over and over, and fell asleep smiling. The nightgown she was wearing was already part of her transformation. Instead of flannel pajamas she had on a sexy nightgown, a sign of the change in her life, still only under the blanket. The next day Eileen woke to a morning of clear desert, the satchel in her hand. She did not share her find with anyone, feeling that it was a kind of gift, a treasure that the Godly presence had sent her.

* * *

When Jeremy returned to the group he looked at her without saying a word, without asking what had happened to her, and said: "I told you so…" Eileen smiled.

The beautiful woman who had recently concluded her fifth decade continued to fight for her new life, for friendships, for femininity. Endless possibilities opened up before her. Some days she felt a decline and others progress, but even the declines gradually diminished.

One evening a man sent her a message, on a website where she was registered, daring for the first time in her life to take a photograph of herself and post it, showing herself as a sexy woman, not only a mother and a successful business woman. Eileen ignored the message. She did not like the man's profile photo, but he was insistent. Eileen answered in short and wrote that she is "not interested and very busy, but maybe she'll have time tomorrow". Several hours later she decided to read the profile of the insistent suitor. Suddenly she froze. His final words were the first words of the poem that she was certain had been written for her, that night in the desert. She ran to the drawer, opened the leather satchel with the sheet of paper… She almost passed out. She could not believe her eyes. Her feelings were confirmed. The words were identical, word for word. Eileen sat by the computer, shaking like a leaf, at a loss at what to do. But still, she didn't like the photograph. All aflutter, the message appeared once more. Eileen decided that it must be her fate. She agreed to meet the man the next day...

About two months later, Eileen introduced her suitor to Jeremy. He looked at them as he always did, right and left, smiled his charming radiant smile, and said nothing...

Three years passed. Eileen restructured her life with Charlie, her love, the same man at whom Jeremy had aimed his radiant smile.

Jeremy, with his endless empathy, was seriously ill. Eileen felt that something was eating away at the man who had brought light into her life. She prayed for his health, called him from time to time to let him know that she was with him in spirit.

A year passed. Eileen and her love Charlie, on a personal trip to Provence, France, were visiting the enchanting town of St. Paul... The two arrived at a parking lot illuminated by the shining sun. It was noon and they smiled at each other happily and contentedly after a gratifying morning. They were planning to take a walk to a beautiful site that they had visited shortly the previous evening. But then a black cloud appeared in the sky above them, overshadowing their car. Suddenly they were besieged by rain.
That same second, Eileen received a message on her phone... 'Jeremy died'...
She sat in the car, speechless. She turned to Charlie unbelieving, looking at the cloud above them, raining down, and burst out in a tearful deluge of her own.

A week later...
Eileen returned home. Shadow, her dog for the past sixteen and a half years, collapsed. She sat by her beloved dog, took her leave of it tearfully, with her children and grandchildren. She carried the dog in her arms to the veterinarian, to be put to sleep. She kissed its nose and said: "Go my dear dog, go to heaven, and there you will meet a dear man, the man who brought a smile to my lips, hope for renewal, and more than anything, belief in myself. Go to him and tell him that Eileen sent you..."

Occasionally Eileen's grandchildren look at the sky and see, side by side, two glowing stars, one for Jeremy and the other for Shadow.

"The need to change is important, the need to be changed even more so, and sometimes in order to change you need a change of place!"

7

Where is Lorna, my first love?

● ● ●

Their rivalry was unique. It left deep marks on him. In those days their competitiveness was intertwined with his unrequited love for her, the fruit of his young innocence.

They were the two top students in their class in Madrid. No one, not even their teachers, could have said who was best – he or she, Manuel or Lorna. In any case, each of the two made every effort to win the title by the end of the school year. Manuel Forero could not decide whether his unrevealed love for Lorna Fastori was an advantage or a disadvantage. On one hand he felt that his love gave him wonderful energies that stimulated him in all fields of life as an adolescent: in school, in sports, in his youth movement, and in his social life. But the opposite was also true, he experienced disappointing and frustrating rejection, aware that she did not show any feeling for him, of course aside from her passionate efforts to win the title of 'best student'. He told himself repeatedly: 'Lorna has no feelings for you'. He was also bothered by the fact that his close friends knew of his personal feelings for her and her disregard of him. It was his first love, at age 15, and it remained his secret; hidden, one-sided, and forever unrequited.

The years passed quickly, surprising Manuel Gomez (Forero). He lost contact with almost all his friends from Madrid, the Spanish capital, the city where he had been born that he had loved as a boy.

After his short military service his parents were sent to Mexico by a leading Roman Catholic organization. He and his younger sister Ninia joined their parents and he was separated from most of his friends and from his roots. He managed to keep in touch with two of them occasionally. He felt a virtual connection with Lorna from time to time. She never completely disappeared from his memory.

On the eve of his marriage to young beautiful Amanda, daughter of the affluent Mexican Gonzales family, at age 27, he thought of Lorna Fastori, his school days' rival who had ignored him in their youth. He thought of their relationship, and mainly of their lack of a relationship; and this on the happiest day of his life, of all days.

Manuel thought that his relationships with Spanish Lorna and with Mexican Amanda had something in common. It was the primacy of the two opposite loves that crossed and intertwined in his mind and heart that evening, two primal loves in such different situations and circumstances. There were both so meaningful to his life. The opposite sides of these two loves flipped over and over inside him and filled his mind, heart, and soul: the immature versus the mature, the one-sided versus the reciprocal, the virtual versus the real, the Catholic youth movement versus the commercial movement of money, rootedness versus artificiality, Spanish tradition versus global existence, and innocence versus pretended innocence. Everything became mixed up in a cocktail of emotions, a combination of complete happiness in the present and a longing for the past.

Perhaps these mixed emotions arose because he was so happy that evening. He suddenly felt that the joy of that evening was arousing in him a longing for the past. 'Nothing is perfect in life', he muttered to himself and continued: 'Even the happiest moments in life are not completely whole…' Soon he would be led to the altar by the bride's parents, but in the remaining minutes he remembered something he had read a long time ago in a book on wholeness:

'There are some things in life to which you must add the missing piece,
And others with which you must make your peace.
And the more you do both
The more you will be at peace with yourself…"

The wedding was joyful and magnificent, and from the moment the groom Manuel was taken to the altar he devoted himself to his bride and his many guests, who including major players in the local business world. From the moment the bride's parents came to collect him from the groom's suite in the magnificent hotel he cut himself off completely from his other thoughts on the night of his wedding, with an emphasis on the night of his wedding... On other nights, immediately following the amazing wedding night, he once again had an unexplained impulse to know what had happened to Lorna, his beloved rival of old. But his strange thoughts of her and of his past diminished and quickly disappeared. Manuel was happy with his married life and felt enriched, both financially and emotionally, in his professional life. Full and rewarding...

o o o

Four years passed in Manuel and Amanda's magnificent villa in the prestigious neighborhood of Armoza in an affluent suburb of Mexico City. But often a quiet period in life is followed by strong turbulence. Sometimes the tempest has a major effect on those who experience it and sometimes it disappears without leaving any significant mark.

Indeed, Manuel was subjected to a storm with an unexpected timing, location, and a figure that suddenly appeared from his past.

The entire commotion began when Pablo Durcal came to carry out an extensive project in Mexico City. A. A. Hospital International, the company he owned, specializing in the planning and establishment of hospitals in developed countries, had won a contract to construct a giant medical center in the Mexican capital.

Pablo, or Pablico as he was called by his school friends, had been in the same class as Lorna Fastori and Manuel Forero. He had also spent a short time with them in a youth movement whose members wore red ribbons on their yellow shirts.

Pablo Durcal was accompanied by a local businessman who represented his firm in Mexico and was his partner in the contract. Together they went to a 'boutique' Catholic church in Armosa for Sunday prayers.

Manuel Gomez (Forero) attended this neighborhood church every Sunday and on Spanish religious holidays. This was his way of remaining connected to his roots and to the tradition in which he had been raised by his maternal grandparents in Madrid.

Manuel was in complete shock when he saw a familiar figure standing beside him in church. Every place in the small intimate Spanish Lights church was close to Manuel's seat of honor.

Manuel and Pablo had enjoyed a good friendly relationship at school and in their Catholic youth movement. Pablo's seat in class, behind Manuel, was very significant. It was a good strategic place for copying answers from Manuel when taking the multiple-answer tests that had been popular at the time. Pablo usually managed to get away with his schemes, and with the help of his passive friend he managed to pass most of his exams. In turn he, the jock, helped his friend Manuel by passing him balls and assists when they played soccer or basketball with rival groups of boys.

But then, in their last year of school, their arrangement failed, and precisely in the most important exam crucial for their further studies. Although many years had passed since then, they both remembered the complication that had probably affected the entire life of Pablo the cheat. Only when he reached the end of the exam did he understand that he had made a mistake and copied all the answers skipping the first. He got all the answers wrong. For example instead of marking answers C, A, D, B, C, A, D he disregarded the first and his answers were A, D, B, C, A, D. He failed miserably. His entire future must have changed as a result and instead of continuing his studies he turned to manual work and became involved in the construction field with a relative who had a successful global firm.

His success in the family firm was meteoric. The story of this exam was one he told his acquaintances at every opportunity. He said that he was lucky that he hadn't managed to copy all the answers from the best student in class… The connection between them, however, had been severed immediately upon graduating.

The two old friends spoke a little about the notorious exam. Rapidly switching topics, Pablo explained to Manuel why he had come to Mexico and how he had wound up here this evening with his local Mexican representative who took him to Sunday prayers where he and Manuel met so unexpectedly.

Pablo was amazed at the story of how Manuel had wound up in Mexico and of his marriage to the millionaire daughter of a prominent family. He also listened to his proud stories of his two year old daughter, a real 'princess'.

The worshippers at the church, most of whom knew and appreciated 'Manuel the Spaniard', felt his excitement at meeting the young stranger with whom he engaged in a passionate conversation. He was not his usual calm and stately self.

The two school friends from the pleasant neighborhood of villas in Madrid sat down on a bench near the church. The Mexican, Pablo's representative, saw that the two were very excited and understood that they wished to speak in private about their past. He told his guest that he would cross the road to his home near the church where he and his wife Carmen would wait to have supper with Pablo.

The conversation between the two old friends, who just the year before had entered their third decade, was exhilarating and aroused memories of their youth in Madrid, Spain. They reminisced and mentioned several friends from that period. And then confident Pablo slapped Manuel on the back and surprised him by whispering in his ear: "Manuel, you must remember your rival and love, Lorna Fastori".
Manuel pretended to be unaffected. He had managed to completely suppress his feelings for the girl although he had not exactly managed to erase her from his life. But he did not understand why. Pablo continued: "I'm sure you'd like to know what happened to her?!"
"Yes, it would be nice to know", he kept up his disinterested attitude. Inside he felt a fire burning within him.
"Well, I can tell you something about her that will probably surprise you…"
Manuel broke out in a cold sweat. "I hope it's a good surprise. By the way, if you tell me that she is the youngest professor at a university in Madrid, or even a senior director in the Department of Education, I would not be surprised… I would be surprised if you told me that at age 31 she has no less than five children…"
"And what if I tell you that just as you were neighbors in Madrid you are neighbors today too…?"
"What do you mean by 'neighbors'? I need some more details… like on those exams, but now you have no one to copy from…"
Pablo found it appropriate to continue joking around with the former A student: "I only copied from you on 'multiple-choice tests', where there was no need to expand and explain the answers but only to mark the correct choices…"
"Still, how are Lorna and myself neighbors?" he couldn't restrain himself. He was so excited and eager.
"Believe it or not, Gracia Manuela is living happily on the island of Curaçao in the Caribbean, on your side of the world…"

"You're joking, so close, I can't believe it. How do you know? What is she doing there? Is she married? Since when has she been there? How does she look?..." Manuel showered him with questions, showing his amazement, at the rate of a first-class machine gun.

Devious Pablo, always known for his sense of humor, did not answer the questions, and added another 'bombshell': "She also knows a lot about you..."

"How does she know? Is she having me followed?"

"Your grandfather, who passed away a year ago, was in the same room in the Saludos hospital as her grandfather, and before he died he told your grandfather how much he misses you and what a wonderful Mexican woman you married four years ago..."

"Pablo, how do you know all these things? Are you in regular contact with Lorna and she has been telling you everything?"

"Yes, for the past six years we have been in close contact... Manuel, you must remember my surname...?"

"Durcal".

"That's it. For the past 6 years it has also been Lorna's. Lornita Durcal. She looks great. She's the mother of our 4 year old son Juan... She manages the ancient library of Spanish books and writings on the island of Curaçao, where we have been living for the past three years. Yes, there is such a thing. The library is beautifully preserved... Next month you are invited to come with Amanda and your two year old daughter Luana to be our guests ...

By the way, my Lornita still has the poem that you wrote her in the eighth grade and I think that I may even remember it.

I'll try to recite it for you:

'Lorna,
You are the loveliest rose,
From your head to your toes.
Although rivals in our class,
Maybe we can love each other at last...
I can feel our hearts beating together
With our love it would be even better.'

Manuel was speechless. He was completely shocked.

"Tomorrow morning I have to fly back to Curaçao so we'll leave the rest of our stories for your Easter visit..."

"One last question, Pablo. How did you become the owner of such a big global project-oriented corporation at such a young age?"
"It's very simple. We inherited the business from Lornita's grandfather who founded it 55 years ago and passed away recently. Until his death I worked with him for seven years after completing my military service. He taught me a lot."

Manuel, his wife Amanda and their young daughter Luana, spent the next Easter on the island of Martinique in the Caribbean. It took Manuel Gomez (Forero) only one day after his incredible meeting with Pablo Durcal to erase Lorna completely from his memory. Of course, her husband, his childhood friend, had helped unknowingly... Now Manuel felt even happier and more liberated than ever, thanks to the surprising encounter at his neighborhood church.

In Curaçao Lorna was amazed by her husband Pablo's story of his incredible meeting with Manuel in Mexico City. She was not at all disappointed that their relationship had not been renewed.

Manuel Gomez (Forero) and Lorna Durcal (Fastori) repressed their joint childhood memories. They continued to do well in all their endeavors... and surprisingly were (relative) neighbors in the same part of the world, without ever seeing each other again... and without wishing to...

'Some situations need the missing piece, and with some we must make our peace and then we will be at peace with ourselves!'

8

Enchanting song in Yangon

● ● ●

66 year old Valentina Bonvini, a retired employee of the Ministry of Education in Rome, wife of Marco, never understood where her 'wonderful husband', as she called him, found the energy for his repeated attempts to realize an obsessive childhood dream. For nearly ten decades he had been doing everything, everywhere, at any time, and in all circumstances, to try and become something that he was not. This occupation was very out of character for him, her husband, the professor of archeology, an esteemed man with an extensive professional reputation.

This obsession to realize his eternal dream often embarrassed Valentina. It happened when her husband tried his luck at social and family events, at meals with his foreign guests, at sing along evenings and parties to which they were invited. These embarrassing attempts even took place at the graduation ceremonies of two of their children from university, one of whom graduated with honors in the computer sciences.

Marco, four years older than his wife and still active in his profession, always tried to appease his wife after embarrassing her with his off-key singing, sometimes in the company of respectable people. He would say to her, usually stroking her face: "My love, singing is good for me, and anyways no one is perfect, with your exception of course my love". When she found his off-key singing particularly embarrassing for her and for others around them his wife would answer: "People are more afraid of being embarrassed than they are of death; death is a certain eventuality, but they hope to avoid being embarrassed".

Whenever she cited this saying he would answer her: "Singing makes me happy, and I'll tell you the truth, I prefer an abundance of happiness to happy abundance…" He further defended his singing and said: "Embarrassment is a subjective feeling. Anyone who loves me will accept me for who I am".

In a lengthy interview broadcast on prime time national channels in Italy, focusing on his impressive archeological discoveries, the complimentary interviewer asked him of his childhood dreams. He promptly answered: "I always wanted to be a birdwatcher and a singer. Someone who studies birds and someone who sings before an audience."

"And what has remained of those two dreams?" The interviewer continued.

"I still dream of becoming a singer…"

"And what about the second dream?"

"I'm not a birdwatcher, but I am free as a bird. So I sing whenever I feel like it, and continue to envy the birds."

In his basic training in the infantry, as a young man on a military base near Bologna slightly more than fifty years ago, he had felt closest to realizing his dream of becoming a singer. During the grueling training routine, he would sing and hum to himself under his breath to keep his spirits up.

The soldiers sometimes heard him singing, when he was slightly more vocal during long runs or in the common shower. The new recruits enjoyed hearing his songs, which they liked.

They did not care about the quality of his voice, or whether the tune was faithful to that of the original song. They were happy to hear the songs of their favorite singers, and the words he sang were exactly those of the original songs. Marco sang in Italian, English, and occasionally Spanish. He knew all the words to every song he sang and never got a single one wrong.

Marco learned English from the songs' lyrics and did well in this language at high school. He learned the words to the Italian songs from his mother, Regina, formerly an Italian dancer, who loved music and singing. She too, to say the least, was not the best of amateur singers…

The soldiers in his unit asked him to sing for them at the end of their basic training. At the farewell party he sang various Italian songs that had won prizes at the San Remo Festival, and tried his best to sing songs in English, those of Elvis, Cliff Richard, Paul Anka, the Platters, and others as well.

The soldiers and commanders enjoyed his 'show', they had a good time. His comrades seemed to melt at romantic songs such as 'Roberta', 'Are you lonesome tonight' and 'When the girl in your arms is the girl in your heart'. The soldiers, who had not been home for a month, began dancing with their rifles, even with the heavy machine guns some were holding. At this moment Marco, 'Marcito' as he was called by his family and friends, felt that he would realize his dream and become a singer…

However, that's not what happened. It couldn't have. Not with his voice and with his far-from-perfect musical ear.

Nonetheless, Marco continued to dream of being at least an amateur singer and went on trying his luck over the years. He was not very successful in these attempts.

For example, he was weeded out of a talents' program held by a radio station in Rome for ages 40+, a program called 'Its never too late', at the first stages. In one incident his children took the microphone away from him when he began to sing at his 55th birthday party.

Marco's wife, Valentina, who loved and appreciated him, tried to protect him from the banter aroused by his singing. So much so, that once she even threatened to leave a party if her husband did not stop singing. But although he went on she did not follow through on her threat. In another embarrassing incident, it was the owner of the karaoke club in the entertainment quarter of Rome who asked the 'proffesoro' to leave the singing to others. So continued his Sisyphean struggle to realize his dream until he had passed the age of fifty.

The Bonvinis took the vacation of their dreams to celebrate Marco the husband 's 70th birthday.

For several years he had been free of his obsession, singing only to himself, quietly, and not in the presence of others. Valentina his wife felt relieved. He felt that he had overcome the crisis of his delusion of being a singer, even an amateur one, and had become occupied with various professional and personal activities that filled his life and silenced his dream, although not completely.

He was very busy with the archeological discoveries he led professionally in areas with antiquities in the Balkans. He was interviewed by the global media on fascinating archeological finds that he had managed to uncover. It was also important for him to go on several fascinating private trips abroad, planned with his wife Valentina.

One trip for which they had planned excitedly was to Myanmar, i.e. Burma. It had always been a dream of theirs.

The active professor and the retired educator landed in Yangon, the biggest and most important city in Myanmar. They were still accustomed to its previous name, Rangoon. A tall and impressive guide who towered above all the other Burmese in the gloomy neglected airport had come to welcome them. The guide held aloft a sign in English saying 'Prof. Marco and Valentina Bonvini, Italy'.

From the first moment at the airport they fell in love with John their guide who spoke perfect English and wore authentic clothing. He was the same age as the visiting man, an affable man with a wide smile. The guide had once headed a popular department at the University of Rangoon (Yangon) but had been fired, accused of inciting students against the cruel dictatorial regime.

John guided the couple in Yangon. They admired its temples, markets, the Muslim Quarter with its mosques. Everything was fascinating and different than what they knew: the impressive buildings from the British era, the amazing hotel from that period where British generals had once resided. Acute poverty was evident in the neglected streets and alleys of the city while in other places incredible wealth could be found, contrasting with the poverty and destitution. There were a few shops with high-class western brands that you would not expect to see in Burma, side by side with delicatessens offering delicacies from all over the world.

After three days the Bonvinis left their guide, John Wing. They flew to incredible awesome destinations, such as Mandalay, Bagan with its hundreds or maybe thousands of temples, the Inle lake with its floating temples, and other impressive places. Marco and Valentina were happy. They could not contain their joy. Human and cultural abundance, colorful markets, folklore shows, villages of stilts on the water. Two dreamy weeks fulfilled the couple's dream. Marco sang to himself with the guides in their small vehicles and sometimes also at tourist sites. The guides and the drivers admired his singing, and with typically shy Burmese politeness they asked for 'encores'. He was happy to oblige and he remembered the last time he had been asked for an 'encore' in basic training.

Valentina called this time in their life 'a once-in-a-lifetime trip '.

When they landed in Yangon 11 days later the charming unique guide once again welcomed the couple at the airport wearing a long skirt.

The last day, spent in a complex viewing Yangon's endless golden temples, was like saving the best for last. Marco and Valentina were amazed at the complex, full of admiration and exclamations. They were ecstatic. The professor was extremely happy. It was the best way to celebrate his seventy years. And he went on singing. To himself.
John Wing was their private guide of the Shwedagon complex. He had fallen in love with the couple and with the singing of 'Mister professor' as he called him, having enjoyed the western culture available in Burma in the 1950s and '60s. He related that he had read John Steinbeck's book, 'East of Eden' in English 23 times (!!). He said that he used to know every word by heart.

John, the charismatic and impressive guide, had felt a connection to the repertoire of western songs that Marco had been humming to himself from the first time he met them. They reminded him of his youth when his country was a democracy and open to the enlightened world, unlike the present. Suddenly, facing the main temple, the Schwedagon pagoda, adorned with more gold that the dozens of other temples in the complex, Marco began to sing. He was aroused by the beauty that met his eyes. He felt that he had undergone an illumination. John enjoyed the singing immensely, not caring about the quality of the singer's voice or the original tune. Marco began to sing the Platters' 'Only you', a song he had learned at an American university in the 1960s. John Wing, the impressive guide, stopped him and asked for a moment's pause… and then, a minute or two later, he found the song that the 'professor', as John called him, was singing, on his mp3.

To the amazement of Valentina, they both burst out in a spontaneous duet. John said that in his youth the Platters had been his favorite group, and 'Only you' was the song that he sang to his girlfriend Anne, who was of British descent. She was captivated by the song and by John who sang it to her fifty years ago. Anne died five months ago. They had been married for half a century, fifty years of marital bliss, producing three children and eight grandchildren. All his children fled Burma when their father was dismissed from the university and even arrested for two months. Today John lives on his own and enjoys guiding tourists from all over the world.

John, formerly head of department at the local university, and Marco, the active professor of Italy and the Balkans, increased the volume of their singing opposite the main golden temple. They worked each other up. In those moments, singing their favorite song expressed a craving, a deep need. The playback from John's device accompanied their voices. Their singing, together with the recorded music, began to attract tens of worshippers who had come to pray at the temples on this day. In a short time, they became surrounded by hundreds of visitors and worshippers. Many of them hummed along with the Italian professor and the Burmese tourist guide. They both loved the song so much, and the large crowd was drawn to them. They sang on and on with the incessant playback, accompanied by the masses of worshippers who joined in. Suddenly the singing acquired the sound of a religious mass. There must have been over one thousand men and women standing outside the temple, the large majority Burmese and also several tourists who admired the spontaneous sight. Some even recognized the familiar song, which had suddenly become a 'popular' mass in the holy and enchanting heart of restricted Yangon.

Professor Marco Bonvini realized the dream of his life in Yangon.
Retired Valentina, who had been an educator for decades, was amazed, and told her husband that she loved and admired him more than ever. She stressed 'more than ever' and not 'as ever'.
The guide, John Wing, told them that it was one of the happiest days of his life.

• • •

The Bonvinis celebrate the Burmese Independence Day annually at home with friends and relatives.
They closely follow in the media political developments in the country that captivated them.

Marco and Valentina enjoy watching the video clip of the prayer 'mass' 'Only you' with the many worshippers opposite the golden temple in Yangon.

A photograph of the couple and the guide, taken by one of the dozens of tourist photographers at the temple complex (for three or five US dollars) occupies prime place on the main wall of the Bonvinis' living room, in their well-kept apartment near the Spanish steps in Rome. The same photograph exactly has a place of honor in John Wing's study.

The charming tourist guide from Burma, who has passed the age of 70, is enjoying a professional boom after years of occupational decline. A steady flow of friends and acquaintances of the Bonvinis who have been coming to Yangun, which is slowly opening up to the world, insist that only John Wing should guide them in Yangon, relating its fascinating history through its golden temples, churches, mosques, colonial buildings, and even a single synagogue.

A digital studio produced a single CD of the song sung by the Italian professor and the Burmese guide in Yangon. It was produced in 200 copies, which Marco Bonvini happily distributed to all his friends. He sent the first copy to his close friend, John Wing, in Yangon, the city that began opening up to tourists. The cover of the CD proudly proclaims: "Singer... Only you... Yangon"...

Everyone must realize a dream, or at least realize that they have one. Dreams can be realized at any time or place. Sometimes a well-loved song is worth a thousand dreams!

9

The exotic woman on the train from Frankfurt

● ● ●

He observed the beautiful young lady travelling on the local evening train slowly proceeding from the busy station in cosmopolitan Frankfurt to its final station in pleasant conservative Wiesbaden, a quiet city with magnificent soul nourishing gardens and famed body pampering baths. Johann hoped within him that the older woman who kept up a constant chatter with the passenger beside her would disembark at one of the intermediate stations and leave her alone, facing him, one on one, an exotic dark young woman with a sunflower perched in her hair. Johann was in a 'don't feel like being alone tonight' mood. Only a short while ago he had taken part in a concert of Jewish music at the concert hall of a Frankfurt university. He had come as a guest of the organizers and the soul tunes he played on his clarinet had been a major part of the festive event.

Frankfurt did not agree with Johann and he was travelling to spend the night at a good hotel in the nearby tranquil city of Wiesbaden. His parents had taken him on a vacation in this city as a 14 year old teenager. And now, 15 years later, he was returning as a clarinetist with a promising musical future, so he believed. The clarinet was half his world. The other half was divided between other varied areas and occupations such as reading, travelling the world, playing chess, volunteer activities, and even

Chinese cooking. As a musician with a deep soul and a big heart he would often perform at hospitals for children with incurable diseases. He played the instrument that was the 'love of his life', as he called the precious clarinet almost always by his side, for those ill-fated children. And now, on the train, the silvery instrument lay folded in its black bag, the same instrument that had only recently helped him arouse the enthusiasm of students and lecturers at the art school campus of the Frankfurt university. Johann found his courage. He turned to the young woman facing him, speaking at the exact moment when the clumsy elderly woman paused for several seconds from her constant tiring patter to take a sip of the cranberry juice she took out of her ragged purse. He spoke in German to the exotic young lady who seemed quite tired out by the monotonous chatter of the old woman: "Excuse me, I'm curious. May I ask whether the language you are speaking is Turkish?!" He addressed only the young lady, assuming that the old woman was not paying attention. He was right.

The young lady played along with him and a smile appeared on her face. She nodded in the affirmative and also confirmed in her pleasant lilting voice that they had indeed been speaking Turkish.

Johann felt that her cute smile was more than a mere sign of courtesy…

They had already passed five stations when two things happened simultaneously. One seemed unfortunate but the other left a hint of something mysterious that might result in some good.

The first thing had to do with the fact that the clumsy woman with her endless chatter did not disembark, rather remained seated and continued to occupy the young lady with idle talk, at least that's how it seemed.

The second, encouraging event was that the exotic woman remained on the train to Wiesbaden as well. Johann, whose parents had started to pester him with questions about 'being married to the clarinet', remembered the man who had conducted the noon concert, who repeated the word 'utilization' three or four times. "Every situation", said the German moderator passionately, "can be utilized as an opportunity". That's exactly what Johann felt now in these circumstances with the young lady sitting near him in the same train car.

They were only two stops away from the final stop at the spa city that reminded him of his youth, with his German Jewish parents who for years would travel to the health and vacation cities of Wiesbaden and Baden Baden.

He remembered that his father had voiced his own doubts at these relaxing trips to Germany and would say to him: "Johann my only son, memory is bound in fear – forgetting requires courage!"

He felt that he would need the few minutes left until they reached the final stop to utilize (yes, 'utilize'…) her smile, find his courage, and take advantage of the opportunity given him after the musical elation on campus. He needed several minutes to develop a conversation with the young lady, who had awarded him her promising smile, or at least so he felt. And then the train stopped at Meinz, the stop before the last. The old woman picked up her purse and packages, took her leave of the young lady with a nondescript nod… and the latter remained seated, sending a shy smile, slightly embarrassed, to the stranger opposite her. The five remaining minutes until they reached the final stop at Wiesbaden reminded Johann of Frank Sinatra's legendary song, 'Give me five minutes more', a favorite of his parents, one that he had played and dedicated to them in a swing beat. They were responsible for encouraging him to learn to play the clarinet, a musical instrument with Jewish overtones which reminded him slightly of his faith. They always enjoyed the music played by their beloved son. He said the name of the song under his breath and took long seconds to plan his next step with the tanned exotic woman whose shapely body and almond-shaped eyes were repeatedly impressed upon him.

To be sure, he had had a good day on campus: hospitality – music – a sympathetic audience – compliments, and even his favorite foods from home: goulash, rich good kneidlach soup, and various cakes topped by strudel, served as part of the Austrian theme. Maybe that success was a sign that the evening would be successful as well?

For some reason she did not seem Turkish to him, rather from some other Muslim nationality. He knew that his first words now would determine his 'utilization' and his chance of not remaining alone at the Crowne Plaza. Johann also hoped that she would understand his words in English: "The sunflower in your hair is my second favorite flower"…

And it worked… she went along with his plan and asked about his most favorite flower. But he decided to leave her in the dark and keep the answer a mystery. "I'll tell you later on", he said. It seemed a good way of drawing out her curiosity.

He continued to develop the conversation about the sunflower - both sun and flower, a winning combination. Opportunities should not be missed and certainly not an exotic woman with a sunflower glowing in her hair. Each of these two components of the flower's name could be used to develop the conversation. He had so many stories about flowers. The young lady, in her few words and her body language, emanated a contrasting sense of shyness and self-confidence. He enjoyed the contrast.

Johann knew that the train would be stopping in two minutes. 'Should I tell her a story about a flower and end it on the platform? Is she a girl who likes stories or does she like short, direct sentences?' he wondered to himself. In that context he remembered that hours earlier, at the end of the concert with the 'utilizing moderator', he had had a rousing conversation with the dean of the Faculty of the Humanities, who had attended the concert and complimented Johann on his engaging music. Johann said to the German dean: "It's all a matter of attitude", to which the latter answered: "True, but you must take a different attitude with each person. That has been my motto for years with the faculty lecturers and that is how I try to adapt myself individually to our multicultural students who come from different countries, including your own".

Johann chose the first approach and offered to tell the young lady an enchanting story about a sunflower held by an American girl as a sign of identification when she came to meet an American marine to whom she had been writing. The young lady agreed to listen to Johann's story and they went to look for a hot drink. She said to herself: 'I wonder what will happen to me with the handsome man, the storyteller, who seems quite classy. He's definitely a fascinating storyteller…'.

She had been on her own for six months now, following her dramatic and courageous step, against all logic, in defiance of her large controlling family and against all odds. She knew that in her ethnic group she was considered irregular, both in her life style and in her outlook. She also knew that two of her five brothers could make her life physically unbearable, in light of her unusual action considering their family and tradition.

The two took a short walk from the train station to his hotel. He suggested the place because when arriving last night he had noticed the pleasant bar with its special atmosphere in the back of the lobby. She, Katrina as she had chosen to be called since coming to Germany, smiled to the bartender who identified her by name.

Johann continued the story of the sunflower, the girl, and the marine. The young lady was enthralled by the story. Suddenly, in the space of one minute, two men identified her by name and said "good evening", one after the other.

"Let's pay and go somewhere else, I don't feel comfortable here", she said to him, her hot cider untouched on the bar. "I know too many people here from my job and I don't feel comfortable being seen with a stranger". Johann felt the level of mystery rising. His attraction to her rose but also his uncertainty about who and what she was and what she meant by 'my job'. Johann was undecided and asked himself whether he would do well to remain with her.

Katrina was quick to understand his thoughts and his distrust in her in those moments and she said to him, "I can see that you have doubts about being with me... my easy consent to come to the hotel bar with you, the men who know me, my sudden wish to leave, and my revelation to you a few minutes ago about being a Kurd. Not German, not even Turkish, rather a Kurd from my people's region in Turkey. But I am willing, on this cold evening, to take a risk and invite you to my modest apartment up the hill. Now the decision is yours. I am willing to take the risk and open my home to a stranger. You are full of doubt and do not know me..."

She took a deep breath: "Will you come with me, or is this goodbye..."

Johann looked at her, cleared his throat from Wiesbaden's autumnal evening cold, looked at the sunflower in her hair that had begun to blow in the wind, and said: "It's not for me..."

Katrina took her right hand out of her coat to shake his and take her leave but then he continued: "It's not for me to lack courage, it's not for me to miss out on utilizing an opportunity that may never repeat itself... and it's not for me to betray my intuition... I'll come with you to your home on the hill!"

It was a small and welcoming apartment, untidy but pleasant. Pictures by Kurdish artists as well as others adorned the walls, complemented by posters with views of Turkish Kurdistan. On the table in the kitchenette there was a tall pile of books and about ten CDs placed on top of each other. He couldn't see the titles of the CDs, and saw the title of only one German book, when Katrina grasped his hand and asked: "What will you have to drink in my little piece of heaven?"

Johann, who felt much more confident with her now than at the hotel bar, answered: "Coffee with a Kurdish aroma!"

"You can have the aroma without the coffee", Katrina surprised herself by answering daringly, a tone she had never before used since fleeing her husband and leaving the magnificent villa where she had lived with him during their 18 months of marriage.

"Now tell me your story".

"I chose freedom. I fled a rich and violent husband, who amassed his fortune in questionable ways. I went through 555 nightmarish days and nights beginning from the night of our wedding. I counted every day, every night; endless days of threats by my brothers, my uncles, and Akram the scoundrel who had the questionable title of being my 'husband', the result of an accursed arranged marriage. Everyone threatened my life if I left him. I managed to escape after signing a legal agreement to take only one small suitcase with personal items, no jewelry or other valuables, and disappear, relinquishing all claims and demands... I gave a place of honor to my favorite CDs. One of them was recorded by my favorite artist and I listen to it every night. It gave me the strength, the faith, and the energy, to survive the long days of beating and vomiting and, to this very day, to believe and to resist my entire family. Three years ago, even before my forced marriage to the scoundrel, it was my employer who invited me to a concert featuring your Austrian compatriot, I am his biggest fan... Would you like to hear the CD?"

"Yes. With the coffee, the Kurdish aroma, and the beautiful woman in your wonderful little bedroom. Let's see if we can find our way there."

In his entire adult life Johann had never experienced such wild creative sex as he did that night.

But even more than his astonishment at the personal and sexual revelation of Katrina the Kurdish-Turkish German he was amazed when their foreplay was accompanied by a CD of his music teacher, a respected musician who had become extremely popular in Germany. Here in the small apartment on the outskirts of Wiesbaden, in this unexpected intimate situation, the virtuoso from Vienna, whom he so admired and to whom he owed his love of the clarinet and his occupation and the joy of his life, suddenly emerged.

She felt incredibly light at the end of the amazing act.

"What do you say...?"

"About being together, the sex, or the music?"

"Begin with the music... and before you say anything I'll tell you that I have a fantasy to own a CD of a clarinet piece I once heard performed by another artist, which reminds me of my approach to life. You must be acquainted with his vocal performance..."

"Is he too an Austrian artist?"

"No. He acquired his fame by playing the song of a great American duo who brought it from the Andes in Peru, telling the story of miners in an underground mine who wish to be free eagles and not caged birds; to be hammers and not nails, to reside in nature and not on a street. I may be inaccurate, but it is definitely a song about the longing for freedom..."

"Katrina, how do you know all these words in English?

"From the nursery school where I teach, caring for the children of diplomats and other foreign residents, including envoys, branch directors of foreign companies. At the nursery school I tell the young children stories and arouse their imagination, teach them values and impart knowledge. The two men who greeted me in the hotel bar send their children to my nursery school and have not heard of my relatively recent divorce, and that's why I was not comfortable sitting at the bar with you, a stranger".

"And what do you wish for this evening, one so amazing for both of us?"

"To feel like an eagle that spreads its wings to endless freedom and to hear this magical song..."

"'El condor pasa'? Is that the song you mean?!"

"Wow. How did you know?!!!" It had been a long time since she had given such a shout.

"Shut your eyes because I have a little surprise for you".

"But I've already shut my eyes this evening, at the height of our pleasure, and sensed unsurpassable surprise when I felt you deep inside me".

"So take another breath and you'll have another one".

Katrina did as he said.

Johann slipped into the small living room, took the pieces of the clarinet from its case and fitted them together.

In his underwear he returned to the bedroom, this time not alone. He stroked her hands covering her eyes, and began playing 'El condor pasa'. Katrina opened her eyes. It seemed that at that moment none of the seven billion people on earth was happier than her. And surely none was more amazed.

It was a rare moment in her life when 'blows' of joy rained down on her, and not only blows...

"One moment, Johann, you owe me something from the train platform where we stood so long ago. So what is your favorite flower?"

"Oh, yes. That's how it began. It's the tulip. But I love it with you in a duet, 'tulips' – 'two lips'.

"I'm lucky that there are so many English speaking foreigners at the nursery school."

"It's also fortunate that you speak Turkish."

● ● ●

The coming Autumn brought the Freimans great joy. Father Johann and mother Katrina celebrated their fourth loving anniversary with their three year old son Herbert, a child who at this young age was already a rare combination of wisdom and beauty, the fruit of such a unique and challenging love.

Johann continued to visit Frankfurt and Germany as a guest at concerts, performing soul clarinet solos. Katrina managed a nursery school for diplomats' children in a high-class neighborhood near her home in Salzburg and was widely appreciated by the parents.

Katrina, who only became more beautiful in time, appeared all over Austria as a popular lecturer with her life story: 'Big courage'. She loved to take her son Herbert along with her when she could.

When Johann was available he liked to come with her and to accompany her story with soul tunes played on his clarinet, always ending with that tune from Peru, of the miners who prefer to spread their wings and be free: 'El condor pasa'.

It is worthwhile to have courage and to pay a high price for freedom, as well as to have the freedom to find courage!

10

Something strange happened at the lovely park

● ● ●

Some things in life feel 'too good to be true'. That's exactly how Victor felt about what happened to him that week with Mary. He tried to find the 'catch' in his inexplicable good fortune.

It all began with a popular dating website. On Sunday night a woman accessed his profile on the website. She saw his photograph, read the information he had given, thought that he looked handsome and certainly seemed like someone who could be suitable for her. 'It's worth a try', she said to herself, and promptly 'tweeted' and sent him an e-mail, suggesting that they speak on the phone.

She wrote to him that two things in his profile had drawn her attention. One was the saying he had posted, 'the present is a present'. The second point that had attracted Mary's attention was his statement that 'one essential condition for meeting someone is that I should not see her picture until we meet... I would like to form my own personal impression of her and of her appearance. Until we meet I would like to imagine her as she describes herself to me on the phone'.

Mary wrote to him that she had not posted her photograph on the website but before they meet, if they so decide, she would be glad to describe herself to him – any part of her appearance that he wished. She added that in her opinion he would 'not be disappointed' when he met her.

Victor read her e-mail. He liked her straightforward approach. He liked direct women. An hour after receiving her e-mail he called the number she had sent him. She was surprised but also admired his promptness. They had an interesting and intriguing conversation, although not too passionate, lasting about 20 minutes. He felt good that the conversation had not been too lengthy. The picture he had formed justified a meeting, at least judging by her description of herself and the contents of the conversation, but did not create exaggerated expectations that often lead to disappointment. His rich experience with blind dates as a single man had taught him that this was a balanced and ideal situation prior to a first date.

Mary and Victor agreed to meet the next evening at an intimate café known to both of them. The conversation between the two flowed easily over glasses of orange juice. Her appearance was not to his taste. She did not seem attractive to him, although she was an interesting and knowledgeable woman. She did speak and behave candidly but he was not completely convinced that she was not only direct but also honest. He was not attracted to her at first sight, although she was quite pretty from an 'objective' point of view (if there is such a thing…). There was no initial attraction and her body language only reinforced his immediate intuition that she was not the woman he is seeking.
They spoke of her life and his life, professional and social occupations, personal and family histories, about their divorces and ex-spouses, and more.
He told her about a meaningful relationship that had ended and then she muttered something inexplicable under her breath, saying "that's something I can't tell you about". Her words left a trace of vagueness, maybe she had not had a meaningful relationship in a long time, and maybe she does now and it has not reached its end, or perhaps she can't say whether it has ended or not. He did not pressure her to clarify her words, as in any case he had no intention of seeing her again.

She interpreted their date of over an hour, quite a lengthy time for a first date, as indication of his wish to continue the relationship. He had not been in a hurry to leave, however, for three reasons. These had to do with his general well-formed approach to life:

One, he believed that anyone with whom you have interpersonal or other contact is worthy of your attention.

Two, 'in the current cosmic and open era', he would say, 'sometimes we go in search of donkeys and find a kingdom'.

The third reason was linked to the second: He believed that 'Good, sometimes even very good, can be found in anything bad…' "Even in this date", he said to himself…

They shook hands and said goodbye and she said that it was a pleasure meeting him.

He replied: 'It was interesting for me too'.

She didn't understand, or maybe didn't want to understand that using the word 'interesting' was his way of ending the relationship. Usually in such situations this word is used as a sign of politeness and lack of enthusiasm.

48 hours, two whole days, are a long time to resume your life, lacking any phone call, e-mail, 'tweet', or SMS, after a first date. Mary decided to act as befitting her straightforward attitude…

Two days after they met Victor received an e-mail from Mary: "You don't like me, and I don't know why. You said that I am pretty, interesting, and knowledgeable, not like most other women you met since your divorce, and I believe that you meant every word. By the way, I completely agree…

In any case, understanding that we are through, and not wanting to 'waste' you on anyone else, I would like to introduce you to a good friend of mine… I believe that you will be captivated by her inner beauty and that you will fall in love with her external beauty".

Victor liked her honesty. It reinforced his initial impression of her forthrightness. He appreciated her candidness, and even more so her impressive ability to come to terms with reality. In this context he remembered that he had always told his employees at the development division he managed in a successful organization:

'There are three levels of rising:

Rise

Raise

Overcome

And in face of Mary's ability to forge on and her other good qualities he was sorry that he was not attracted to her. What a shame.

He thanked her by e-mail for her altruistic and generous offer to introduce him to her good friend, with the warm descriptions of her inner and outer beauty. He also sent her the words about overcoming.

From here on things began to develop at a rapid and surprising pace…

Victor called Mary's friend that very evening. He received a good impression of her from their conversation, as she did of him. She wanted to e-mail him her photograph. But he asked her not to, following his rule. "If a 'blind date' then blind it shall be", he would say to himself.
They made a date to meet the next day in a lovely park they both knew and loved, midway between their homes.

This special park housed an art gallery, a beautiful lake with a romantic gondola in the center, and a pleasant café and restaurant on the lake, illuminated romantically in the evenings. Both felt that their choice of place, at least, was a good one. This time he deviated from his 'measure of prior expectations' as his conversation with the woman, Carol, was longer and more emotionally charged than usual, in his experience from previous blind dates. Her description of her external appearance, at least as she presented it, was to his liking, and complemented his positive impression of their conversation.

Throughout the twenty minute ride to the lovely park the sentence 'too good to be true' was on Victor's mind. A combination of a rejected woman who overcomes her disappointment and introduces him to someone she defines as an impressive friend, with whom he had an intriguing and even tempting conversation. Soon he would meet her…

At precisely 8 pm Victor was at the gate of the park, exactly when and where they had arranged. Carol, his 'blind date', arrived two minutes later and approached him. That moment he understood that Mary had played a trick on him…

It took him only a second to say to himself: "Victor, you knew that it was 'too good to be true'". The woman was fat and clumsy, quite an eyesore, to say the least. Her appearance was unkempt. The moment she arrived she said "Victor?" and he replied, hardly concealing his annoyance: "No, Ma'am". He felt ashamed, even humiliated, by the fact that he had agreed to meet the rejected woman's friend. 'It was quite obvious', he chastised

himself, at least happy that he had safely reached the parking lot...
But then a chain of events that happens only once in a lifetime, if at all, proceeded to unfold. What happened that moment at the gate and where it all led Victor is simply unbelievable...

His inner turmoil was dwarfed when he saw a woman who was obviously very agitated wiping away her tears and approaching a car parked near his. He understood that something bad had happened to her, certainly worse than his own unpleasant but bearable experience. He asked her if he could do something to stem her flowing tears. He offered to bring her a bottle of water to calm her and some tissues for her tears from his nearby car. She thanked him and said that he could help by listening.

They were linked by the trauma that both had undergone simultaneously in two different parts of the same lovely park.

They sat in his car and she took a sip from the brimming water bottle. He felt that this was a woman he would have been glad to have met at the gate to the park several minutes ago. She immediately began her story, telling him that she had fled here upset by a big fight with her boyfriend. She grabbed his phone in a restaurant when he looked down to send a text message. She saw messages from his lover. She had suspected him previously of cheating on her with someone she knew. She threw the phone at him enraged, and in tears said 'I'll have nothing more to do with you and this time its final...' As she got it all out Victor felt that he liked her...
He found a way of calming her down and told her about his recent unpleasant embarrassing experience at the entrance to the park.
She became subdued. Felt confident and in good hands. His handsome masculine appearance, strong voice, and way of listening agreed with her. Even the bottle of mineral water this stranger had given her was the best beverage she had tasted in a long time.

She continued to speak of her tough evening at the restaurant... He surprised her by cutting in and asking whether she happened to live in the residential tower on his street, number 14. She answered him, amazed, "yes", and asked how he knew...
Victor surprised her again and told her that to his chagrin he had twice seen her leaving the building in the embrace of a man. He understood that she wasn't available, although he noted to himself that he was

attracted to her combination of female allure and beauty…

She swallowed hard and continued to tell him about herself. She said that she had been single for the past forty minutes for the first time in twenty four years. She had been married for twenty years and for 4 years since the divorce had had a boyfriend, whom she had just left forever less than an hour ago. "What do you think?" she asked and went no further. She stared at him, expecting a personal statement.

He thought once again of the incredible fate that had brought him to gaze at her twice in passion without her knowledge, while with her boyfriend. He cited from memory a suitable saying that he had once read, which seemed appropriate for this encounter with his neighbor from the 24-story building:

'Spaces and distances
Are usually
So close.
This is a saying about people, incredible views
And all parts of life'

Victor felt that this saying was very appropriate. The woman whom he had sought was so close, not in a distant country or another city, not even in a nearby neighborhood or house, but in his very own building…

Suddenly he found her in his arms. Everything developed quite quickly and with a mystic air in this special evening near the lovely park.

As one addicted to wordplays, his luck seemed to extend to the woman's name as well. At the end of the evening in his car, after hugs and kisses that left promises of more to come, and only then, did they tell each other their names. He treated her name, Norma, as a bonus. He asked, rhetorically, if he could use the first letter of her name, N, to summarize the evening, and then said immediately: "Nice, it was very nice to meet you. And you yourself are a very pleasant person. With your permission I will also use the second letter of your name, O, to tell you that I fell that you are my 'one and only'". She liked this play of words.

The romance between Norma and Victor, both divorced and parents of a young child, flourished. It was probably easy for them to meet at his apartment or at hers, living as they did in the same building, number 14, in the city of Albany, New York. Only 5 stories separated them. She lived on the 17th floor and he on the 22nd.

Two weeks after they had met by chance their relationship was advancing at full speed.

He said to her: "Now we've reached the third letter in your name, R. Yes, you with your femininity and 'romantic' personality are like a gushing spring."
And she answered him: "For me, you are the real Victor. Both a victor and real – a real man and lover."
"She has caught on to my wordplays…" Victor told himself happily.

Two more weeks passed, in an atmosphere that included wine, candles, and declarations. Once again he asked her permission to use the letters of her name to send her a message. This time it was the turn of the fourth letter, M. "You are 'magic' for me, magical and enchanting." At the same time, he played the clip 'You've got the magic touch' on his tablet and embraced her strongly. He said: "You are my response to everything; you are my friend, my confidante, my lover, and my girlfriend". He continued this statement with another song in his bedroom, 'You are the answer to my life's dreams' by his favorite singer, Roy Barnet.

Norma's fountain of happiness grew. She replied to him with a wordplay of her own: "You, Victor, are victorious over my tears that are transformed today".
He admired this wordplay, using his name.

After one month he asked her permission, in her apartment, to use one of the letters of her name again, this time the last letter "A", to convey the most important message for both of them. She was very expectant: What is the special word that he wishes to express with the letter A?
"I want you to be my 'address'; I would like to come and live with you".
She continued his gist: "I have an A of my own, 'adore'. I adore you. Yes, of course. I agree and I'm glad that we will live together with our two children…"

It was relatively easy for him to move some of his possessions to her apartment.

A week later, five weeks after they first met, she asked to tell him a secret. She told him that Mary whom he had met, who had deceived him and led to their own encounter, was… the lover of her former boyfriend, the man whose phone she had thrown at the restaurant in the park. It had taken her until today to tell him, Victor, her lover.

"Are you certain?!" Victor asked her in astonishment.

"Definitely… I knew that it would astound you," she wrapped her arms around his neck and drew him to her.

"Now I understand why Mary sounded vague when she said something about a relationship or ending a relationship. Now it all fits."

"And what do you suggest we do with this interesting information, my dear?"

"The most natural thing. Let's send Mary a nice bouquet for the weekend with the following message:

'Thank you Mary for bringing us together!
From:
Victor (thanks to you I came to meet your friend that evening…)
Norma (thanks to you I broke up with my boyfriend, Neil, who cheated on me with you)
And thanks to you we met at the elegant park, when I, Victor, was evading your friend, and I, Norma, was fleeing my boyfriend. Thanks to you we have found the love of our life, and this bouquet of roses is a token of our thanks. But beware of the thorns…"

After that incredible unforgettable evening when the happy couple met, Mary had severed all contact with Carol, her former friend, who had not managed to trick Victor on her behalf at the entrance to the park. She had expected Carol to do her bidding, but that's not what happened, and unluckily for Mary the 'bitch' they did not meet. She felt at the time that her friend had not made enough of an effort to 'scam' Victor.

When they had known each other for about six months, Norma and Victor celebrated 100 birthdays with their many friends. A total of exactly 100. He was 54 and she 46. Their birthdays were a week apart.

A week after this special birthday celebration, entirely by chance, the two former friends, Carol and Mary, happened to meet. It was at a social event, following their complete estrangement.

At first Mary did not recognize Carol. She looked at her, at the pretty thin woman facing her, who had lost over 30 kg. (!) since they last met. She had also taken care of her skin, changed her hairdo, and was dressed fashionably.

"Carol?!!"

"Yes, Mary, its Carol, your former best friend!"

"How did you do it?! You're a 'hot chick', I don't believe it…"

"Do you remember that evening when you sent me to meet a man and told me that it was your act of revenge… and that I would be doing you a favor? And I'm sure you haven't forgotten that you were angry at me for not meeting him. You didn't believe that I couldn't find him and you hung up on me… so that evening, when I too was disappointed that I hadn't met him, I continued from the entrance to the park, where we were supposed to have met, to the art gallery inside. It was the last night of a photography exhibit, showing the drawings and sculptures of women who were exhibiting their works of art, reflecting their transformation from very fat to thin women. The artists photographed, drew, and sculpted themselves before and after the change… I was inspired by the exhibit, entitled 'You can do it too!'…

And then I began to diet, juice diets and others and lots of workouts, as well as beauty treatments. These are the results, as you can see for yourself… It happened thanks to you, Mary, when I arrived at the park that evening and ended up at the exhibit that changed my life. Thank you, Mary!… And I am also involved in a serious relationship."

"And I, Carol, have received lots of thanks over the past week, but I am no longer in a relationship."

"Good luck, Mary. By the way, the lovely park is a wonderful place for new beginnings…"

ɒ ☯ ☯

When Victor ran out of letters in the name Norma, and when they celebrated their first year of joy together, he told her that "Floor 22, your floor, is my lucky number for lotteries and bets…"

She said: "Every day for the past two years, I have felt that I have won the 'Super Bowl' by having you".

Victor responded: "Since we have been together, it is the first time that I can identify with my name. Victor – a 'real victor'. Thanks to you."

To this very day Norma and Victor Simpson live happily with their two children in an affluent part of Albany.

Every two weeks they spend the weekend at that lovely park in Albany, with the gondolas, together with their two children, Sandy and Andy, who became sister and brother in heart and soul, and now share the same surname.

Our love is often so close. This is a message about people, desires, and almost all parts of life.

11

The grandfather, the grandson, and pineapple genetics

● ● ●

It was a night of stormy waves, easily observable from the Davidovs' spacious apartment with its view of the sea. The waves were surprisingly tall and reached the breakwater with their towering spray. Hanan enjoyed the impressive sight from the roof of his immaculate penthouse, where he lived with his wife Nicole. The storm outside was a perfect complement to the inner turmoil and excitement experienced over the past few days by the unique adventurous man looking out at the sea.

Only less than a day ago he had landed in Israel after nine months of volatile business activity in an unstable African country. The sight of the sea and the lights of the Tel Aviv promenade seemed light years away from the jungles where he had been held, mostly against his wishes.

The very next day, Friday noon, Davidov, who was a proud grandfather, had promised to pick up his grandson Matan from kindergarten. He and the child's grandmother were planning to host their beloved 5 year old grandson at their apartment for the weekend.

The thought of spending a weekend with his witty smart grandson and his wife had kept his spirits up while held under house arrest in that accursed African capital. He owed his release to his connections with a prominent ambassador in that country. It had been a false arrest based on a false accusation in the African country where an uprising had put an end to his business.

His Skype conversations with his son, daughter-in-law, and wife, as well as some of his close friends, helped him bide his time until he was able to become reunited with his many relatives and acquaintances in Israel. These conversations helped him get through the tough months of his house arrest. The only thing that bothered him in these conversations was that his son and daughter-in-law would make jokes at his expense and say how amazing it was that there was no external sign of any genetic link between him and Matan his grandson who so misses his grandfather. It was said with the humor characteristic of the young couple, but grandfather Hanan took it very seriously.

Indeed, since Matan was born relatives always noted the surprising resemblance between the boy and his mother Merav and her parents. They also saw a resemblance to his son and Nicole. Even Matan's two cousins resembled the gifted child who fascinated everyone. Hanan himself had always searched for at least one sign that would hint at a genetic link between him, the grandfather, and his beloved grandson. All his efforts were to no avail and to his disappointment he found nothing. Neither in the boy's facial features – the shape or color of his eyes - nor in his mouth, ears, nose, forehead, shape of the cheeks, or color of his skin, or any other body part, was any resemblance evident. The more Grandpa Hanan loved his grandson the more frustrated he became with the complete lack of genetic resemblance to his heir. Even when interrogated in the African capital, Grandpa Hanan had found refuge in thoughts of how to solve the problem of this genetic incompatibility. He decided to utilize all his creative skills for this purpose. 'Something will have to happen to change things', he repeated to himself. 'Even if I have to change my appearance through plastic surgery, or perhaps something more drastic, to change the laws of genetic resemblance...'

He was convinced that a creative solution would emerge once he landed at long last in Israel and saw his charming grandson.

Nicole, the dedicated grandmother with her European manners, prepared a room for the 'little prince' in their apartment, in preparation for the 'royal' visit. Only a red carpet was missing. The grandmother had seen their grandson quite often while her husband was away in Africa.

Her husband had been waiting for this weekend for nine months that seemed like an eternity. Hanan defined this period as 'nine months of waiting'. The grandfather, who looked eight or ten years younger than his 60 years, planned his time with his grandson excitedly: What he would tell him to justify why they had not seen each other for so long; where he would take him, what he and his grandmother would buy for him; what food they would prepare for him. A weekend together would 'compensate' for his travels which had got him into trouble and caused his unexpected lengthy absence.

In his suitcase he had authentic African gifts for his grandson and some children's toys that he had bought at the duty free shops when leaving Israel. He had wooden dolls of seven common African animals in an impressive box.

He had also bought a 3D book with pictures of flowers. He had an impressive box of model trains, and other gifts that would not have embarrassed a small toy department.

Mystically, when Hanan had shopped for his grandson before and after the house arrest, he had felt that the various items would have significance for proving their genetic resemblance. Sounds imaginary? Maybe. But his inventions, which helped double and triple agricultural crops, had also sounded imaginary when first developed. Some were completely unrelated to agriculture, having more to do with physics and even plastic arts. Hanan was known for his creativity, as one who had experienced many strange events throughout his life. Who knows, maybe he had a hand in their occurrence?!

Standing on the balcony of his apartment, watching the foaming waves, Grandpa Hanan found himself challenged to realize his dual fantasy in the first weekend after his adventurous journey: to realize his love for his grandson in real life – not through Skype, and to identify or create a genetic link between them. He would not accept statements that 'there is no external genetic resemblance between Hanan and his grandson'.

As if this was not enough, Hanan Davidov, the man and not the grandfather, was in the midst of another exciting venture, of a completely different kind. It had significant meaning for him and his wife, with potential implications for Matan, their natural heir. In three days, Hanan the businessman was to announce his decision concerning a giant financial project: whether to take up an offer to invest in pineapple plantations in a Caribbean country, in cooperation with a childhood friend who had been living there for some years. The investment required was considerable. The decision might definitely affect his future, either way. There was a big chance of enormous profit, but also the risk of losing his life savings. All this intermingled within the ocean of his thoughts: the close and distant past, the present and the future; distant memories and current decisions, business risks, and even a flashback to falling in love with Nicole, who had certainly turned out to be a successful gamble. This entire cocktail of thoughts and feelings formed a jumble, while he continued to stare out at the breaking waves.

Throughout the last nine months, from his house arrest in the African country to the current moment, he had given much thought to this business decision. His longing for Matan increasingly intruded and inserted itself into his deliberations. Almost like the rapid rate of the waves breaking on the breakwater. And Hanan searched for his own breakwater, one that would break the balance of his tortured doubts, in such a tough dilemma. Should he accept the deal and make the best of a rare opportunity, at the same time risking a considerable part of his wealth and that of his wife, or should he reject the deal, keep their money, and maybe be left with the regrettable feeling that he had missed out?... His unease at the lack of genetic resemblance returned to interrupt these business thoughts...

The meeting with Matan the grandson, after long months of absence, was even more joyous than anticipated. It was extremely exciting. The 'little prince' jumped on his tearful and longing grandfather... Matan yelled: "Grandpa, I couldn't fall asleep all night. Daddy, mommy, and granny promised me all week that you would come back and that I would go and visit you and spend the weekend with you. I told all my friends at kindergarten."
"Can you think of a sentence about you and me?"
"On a sunny day and on a rainy one, I always love Grandpa Hanan!"
"And you my grandson Matan, are having lots of fun." Davidov answered him immediately, like he was playing a fast game of ping pong with his grandson.
Granny pretended to cry and asked Matan for a sentence about her as well, and it took him only a few seconds: "When it comes to Granny Nicole I love it all..."

It took Grandpa Hanan a long time to show his grandson all the presents he had brought with him. First was the box with the seven wooden animals:
"These are the favorite animals in Africa". He had hidden one of them

before bringing Matan home. The grandfather took the six remaining animals out of the box and said/asked: "I want to give you one of them. Which do you like the most?"

Matan examined and touched each of the animals, carved out of the finest wood. The prince seemed disappointed... "Lion, elephant, horse, tiger, zebra, monkey, and that's the last. Too bad..."

"Why are you so sad, Matan, my dearest, because you want all of them?!"

"No grandfather, because my favorite is..."

That moment Grandpa Hanan took the giraffe out of his pocket. "Maybe this one?"

"Yes, yes, grandpa. The giraffe has always been my favorite..."

Grandpa Hanan had been 'checking' to see whether his love of this unusual animal was genetic, and in light of what had happened he felt a slight sense of 'genetic victory'. Hanan Davidov, as a tall boy and teenager, had always been called 'Hanan giraffe' by his neighborhood friends, because of his obsessive love for 'the animal that sees much more than anyone else, that views everything from above,' as he would say. He always liked to take an expansive and comprehensive view of life.

This 'genetic achievement' comforted the grandfather.

More and more presents were opened.

"And grandpa, why is this book so thick?"

"Because every page opens up into a cardboard flower and sounds a tune."

The book had 16 pages of flowers.

Gifted Matan, only 5 years old, already knew the names of about half of them.

Grandpa Hanan gently stroked Matan's dark hair and asked:

"Do you like the book? Which flower do you like the most?"

"Grandpa, I like the cyclamen the best, and I also like to take a rest... and how fun that my family is the best."

Hanan felt on an incredible genetic and spiritual high.

In one sentence his much-loved grandson had created an unbelievable link.

He himself, in his childhood, had been strongly involved with the 'Cyclamen' Scouts group.

Trains were his favorite game and even today when in Europe he loved to travel by train.

At age 8 he had won first prize for a slogan he sent to a children's newspaper for the new drink, Pepli. His slogan was: 'Pepli is our friend, we drink it to the end!' The prize was a two-week family admission to a Jaffa amusement park.

And in his mind Hanan was back in his childhood. Of all the many rides in the amusement park his favorite was riding the bumping boats with his family... But that moment he was abruptly brought back from his childhood memories. Matan hugged Grandpa Hanan and said: "Grandpa, lets continue with the presents later and maybe you can take me sailing on the Yarkon River... it will be fun to bump into the other boats..." Another 'genetic link'...

At the kiosk located at the entrance to the dock on the Yarkon River Matan asked his grandfather to buy him a popsicle. There was a group of children there, returning from an outing on the river. They were eating different flavored ice creams - lemon, strawberry, chocolate, grape, coke, mint, tri-color. Matan asked for a different flavor than those chosen by the other children:
"Grandpa, I'd really like the pineapple popsicle down there, under all the others."
"I'll buy you one, Matan my sweet, if you tell me what you'll do with the popsicle..."
"I'll eat the pineapple popsicle, if you don't tickle...
Grandpa, do you want to have a good time and help me rhyme?"
As a boy and teenager, Hanan Davidov had been known as the king of rhyme. After so many rhyming sentences produced by Matan his grandson, he felt a 'definite genetic victory', as he told himself.

And with this feeling of euphoric happiness he now knew that he would become the 'king of pineapple plantations' in the Caribbean, together with his friend who had arranged the deal. Suddenly the decision seemed so simple, so clear.
Best of all, he knew for certain that the best genetic link was the 'mental' link...
And the best, is eating a pineapple popsicle with the rest. Even if he had 'stolen' the rhyme from his charming smart scion.

The next year of Hanan Davidov's life was a crazy one, after his tortured months under house arrest in Africa. His investment in the pineapple plantations in the Caribbean proved extremely successful. A Chinese foundation investing in agriculture bought out Davidov and his friend for three (!) times their initial investment. The future of Matan and of Vered, his newborn baby sister, was secure, to a large degree thanks to Matan's choice of a pineapple popsicle at the kiosk on the Yarkon River.

And another thing happened at the conclusion of this incredible year in the life of the loving and adventurous grandfather: His book 'Mental genetics is always a winner' topped the bestseller list from the start. The first page said:
"Dedicated to my loving grandson, Matan Davidov, who is the inspiration for this book, and the composer of all its rhymes."

Hanan Davidov had had a childhood dream of writing a mystery featuring policemen, detectives, and crooks.
Matan, a top first grade student, told Grandpa Hanan who came to pick him up after school: "Grandpa, I'd really like to sit across the street on the bench near the police station. I always pass by it on the way to school".
"And what will we do there, Matan, just sit?"
"Of course not, grandpa... We'll both quietly follow the detectives and policemen entering and leaving the station. Maybe we'll also see robbers, crooks, or all kinds of people being arrested. The good against the bad."
"And why shall we follow them? For what purpose, Matan my sweet?"
"We can write a great detective book together, me and Grandpa Hanan forever!"

No grandfather could have been happier than him, certain of 'genetic triumph' with his grandson.
That same moment, Matan hugged his grandpa's neck, immersed in his happiness, and pointed at the sky:
"Look, Grandpa Hanan, what a beautiful rainbow..."
"Wow, I forgot to give you the train game..."
"Let's stay together always and never let go!"

Genetics is evident not only in physical traits. It strongly links generations through emotional and mental qualities.

12

Alexia's fantasies

• • •

Sexy eccentric Alexia truly thought that the two popular Hollywood film stars of whom she constantly spoke were in love with her or at least knew her well. Indeed, in her heart and mind she loved and admired them unendingly. In the inner world she had created for herself she lived the lives of the two. She recited the gossip circulating about them. She was familiar with all details of the films they had featured in, and all their roles in these films. She remembered every piece of information about them that had been revealed in the media. Alexia described her 'relationship' with these two stars to anyone she could, including her sisters, her employer and son, and her neighbors. She gathered news about them from various gossip shows on television and radio of which she was an avid viewer and listener, such as 'Stardust'. Various magazines specializing in Hollywood and the cinema were also an important source of knowledge about the film stars who 'love' her and whom she loves.

Alexia Sopholes indeed fantasized about being part of the glamorous world of the film stars, which was in fact light years, or maybe dark years, away from her real life as a young maid. It was a harmless infatuation. Maybe the opposite; it was a good way to escape the hard life she had been living since a young age and to cope with her need to return home to parents whom she did not love.

Certainly a respectable escape compared to other young women her age from the same rundown neighborhood. Some of them were on drugs, had hooked up with criminals, and two had even begun working as prostitutes at a young age.

While fantasizing about 'contact' with the two film stars, in reality she was a maid. She was employed by the Neris Family in their fabulous villa, from which she could see the slum where she herself lived.

Sixteen year old Manos, the only son of Maria and Antonius Neris, was an introverted boy, not very popular among his classmates and neighborhood friends. He mostly liked to keep to himself. He spent many hours facing the television screen, watching science fiction films and 'devouring' comics that he would buy or obtain wherever he could. There was also a different type of magazine to which he had become secretly attached…

His personal drawers in his room were 'his little patch of heaven'. Manos hid erotic Playboy and Penthouse magazines, and even more daring publications, like Hustler and Porn Today.

Only two people knew about these magazines. The second was Alexia, who had found them several times under his blanket when making his bed.

Alexia, who came from a large poor family, did not have much chance of succeeding in life. Her point of departure was too low. At age 12 she was already helping her mother work to support the family, washing floors and cleaning the private homes of families in an affluent neighborhood of Athens, across the road. She lived with her parents and her four sisters. Her father was a burden on the family and for many years he had hardly worked and spent most of his time playing cards and backgammon for money and drinking ouzo with his friends in a dilapidated rundown café. Surprisingly, the authorities ignored this illegal activity. Once in a while, her father helped his brothers with light portage jobs.

Alexia Sopholes had first come to the fabulous villa of the Neris family nearly a year ago. A relative of her mother, who worked in the high-class suburb, had found her a job with them and she began to work there from 9am to 4pm, five days a week.

She cleaned and polished, organized and arranged, laundered and ironed, washed and dried, and even learned to cook basic foods requested by her strict employer. For the first year her work at the villa was in general a mutual success. Alexia was happy with her job and enjoyed spending all day at the well-tended villa, a real castle for her. Her pay was fair and adequate.

During the first year, her employer felt that in contrast to her two previous maids this time around she had done well to employ Alexia. She had the good sense to remain silent when she heard the fantasies that Alexia told her and her son. At this stage, in the first year, she and her husband saw it as a harmless mental disorder with no effect on the quality of her work. Alexia performed her job well, fulfilling all her responsibilities. The food she made was indeed not always the best, but she made an effort and showed improvement. Manos the son enjoyed the fantasies she described to him as did sometimes his parents and occasional visitors to their home.

Alexia did not know it, but Manos the teenager had fantasies of his own. In his mind and imagination he began to lust after Alexia and to imagine coming into contact with her feminine sexy body.

On the eve of his 17th birthday he decided to realize his fantasies with the sexy maid.

It was a wintry day with thunder storms and lightning. Manos' father was on a business trip abroad and his mother had gone to visit her sick mother on the other side of town.

Manos had the beginnings of a cold and his mother agreed to his plea to stay home from school. At his request, Alexia brought him some chicken soup to his room. They were alone in the house. When she bent down to give him the tray her voluptuous curves tempted him, visible through her low-cut blouse. He found the courage. He could no longer stand the temptation. He surprised her and himself as well…

"Can I hold you to me?"

Alexia, with her lack of distinction between dreams and reality, consented immediately as though she had been waiting for the question all year long, since arriving at the villa.

She held on to him. She did not understand what the hug meant, whether and where it would lead. She had had two previous 'incidents' at the two other homes where she been employed. But there the circumstances had been completely different. The two previous incidents had cost her her job. At the time, and now too, she could not decide whether her unique sexy appearance was to her benefit. Her full lips, attractive butt, ample bosom, erect nipples, and long legs - and all in one woman. 'It's no surprise', she said to herself in moments of fantasy, 'that my film stars love me…'.

From here on, from the hug that rapidly developed into a relationship, the burning snowball was unstoppable. In fact, neither of them wished to put an end to their affair, even if the risks could be seen on the horizon.

Alexia passionately utilized her considerable sexual experience, the product of several years of relationships with two married men at whose homes she had worked in two different residential areas since the age of 16. She had had secret tempestuous sexual relationships with each of them: With one for two years, with the other 18 months.

The first, a well known television personage who knew of her fantasies, had suggested that he contact one of the two film stars she loved and admired. It was his way of seducing her. And she fell for it.

The second bought her gifts and gave her many magazines on Hollywood. In both cases she was the one to end the relationship, because it made her uncomfortable. She discovered that the first man had been leading her on with promises to introduce her to the film star she loved. The second wanted her to have sex with his good friend, a member of a crime gang. In both cases she acquired extensive sexual experience, but felt that the two married men, both over 40, about her father's age, had used her as a sex slave. She preferred to keep her self-respect and work for a living. This was how she had arrived at the Neris'.

The first time Alexia felt an attraction and emotional affinity, beyond the sex, was in her relationship with 17 year old Manos, at the Neris'. It was also the first time that she felt like a sex instructor in the erotic acts rather than a sex slave.

At the time the hidden intimate relationship between teenage Manos and sensual Alexia began, Maria felt that she was no longer satisfied with the maid's work. Her cleaning had deteriorated. Glassware began to break, and even her ironing was less than perfect. Maria's husband complained as well. Moreover, crucial difficulties began emerging in his business. Maria decided to fire Alexia. But Manos took Alexia's side and begged his mother to reconsider and keep her on.

He said that his mother was judging Alexia badly because she was nervous about his father's business situation and her mother's illness. He launched a campaign for several weeks. Alexia knew about it. Mrs. Neris was persuaded by her son's arguments and let her stay on for another six months.

During these six months Manos and Alexia managed to have sex occasionally in secret. For Manos it was a sexual adventure from which he learned erotic secrets that transformed him from a virgin into a real man. For the first time in his life he was happy. For the first time since Alexia had first had sex when she was 16 she enjoyed it and did not feel like an exploited sexual object.

At the conclusion of these six months, Mrs. Neris began to suspect that something was happening between her son Manos and her maid Alexia. She had no proof, but her feelings were clear.
She made a plan to find out. She lied to her son and maid and said that she was going to visit her mother for the day on the other side of town. At the time her husband was abroad, trying to solve his serious business problems.
Alexia and Manos eagerly awaited Maria's lengthy visits to her mother. For a week they had found no way of meeting and of having sex.
Maria tricked them. She did not go to her mother's. She took them by surprise and returned home after two hours, where she caught her son having sex with the maid. She passed out on the spot.
The next day, Manos' mother felt better and Alexia was no longer working at the Neris'.

The relationship between Alexia and Manos did not end. It only changed in nature. They met clandestinely in various places for the next four months.
Manos submitted a request for Alexia to work as head of housekeeping at an international start-up firm, Greek Gen Com, that had opened in the industrial park near his home. Only the two of them knew about it. His letter to them on her behalf was worded temptingly. The director scheduled an interview with her following the letter.
Alexia received a job as the office housekeeper, responsible for cleaning, beverages, and refreshments for guests, and other tasks that elevated her above the level of a mere cleaner.
The small start-up firm employed 15 people, mostly scientists and young Greek computer professionals who had studied abroad and returned to Athens. Their contract stated that they would receive a lower salary than those offered in the market but would own options that could be realized if the firm went public or was sold.

At the age of 23 Alexia was extremely fortunate. Greek Gen Com, active in the field of alternative medicine based on ancient Greek remedies, was sold to an American conglomerate for $180 million. Alexia Sopholes, head of housekeeping, owned options equaling 0.7 percent of the company's value minus its liabilities. She received a tax-free sum of about 400 thousand dollars.

A short while after the publicized sale, on the other side of the road, in the high-class neighborhood, two terrible incidents happened at the Neris': One was that Manos' father, Antonius Neris, went bankrupt, and as a result the family lost all its assets. All their possessions, including the house, were seized.

Even worse was that 19 year old Manos, who had not enlisted in the army, had a serious internal disease. His life depended on undergoing surgery abroad, and the operation and expenses were estimated at $150 thousand. His family did not know when and where they would find the money. They had no access to their money or assets.

And then, at the height of their despair, Alexia knocked on the door, to their astonishment. Rumors of the considerable sum she had received thanks to her work at the successful firm had made the rounds and reached the posh neighborhood.

Alexia and Manos had kept in touch, and their relationship included not only sex but also a hidden romance. They had remained involved even after the sale and up the present, when she came to Manos' parents and offered to pay for the surgery.

They were astounded and could not believe it. They suddenly saw a ray of light in all this 'tragic period', as Maria said. The maid had appeared as a real angel to save their only child, who was also overcoming another health problem that had prevented him from enlisting.

Only they knew how many efforts, miscarriages, and fertility treatments had been necessary until they managed to have their only child.

Alexia Sopholes accompanied Manos Neris to have the surgery. His parents also flew with them to Philadelphia, to see a reputable surgeon who specialized in Manos' rare medical condition, as did a Greek doctor.

The surgery was successful and young Manos recovered.

Alexia Sopholes was interviewed by a local television channel on her unusual human interest story and on how she had donated a significant part of the money she had received for the sale to save the life of her former employers' son.

In the television interview she first revealed her secret affair with young

Manos. She received his prior consent. Many viewers were touched by the televised story. It was aired on a popular channel in Philadelphia, where Manos had had his surgery.

From here on things began to develop quickly, transformed from fantasy to reality:

A well-known producer of national television series, Simon Good, happened to watch the program. He was fascinated by the incredible young woman interviewed.

The next day he found out the telephone number of Alexia Sopholes and suggested that she appear in a new television series he had been planning: 'Tempting maids'. She would speak in Greek and be dubbed in English.

Alexia was astounded by the producer's offer. Excited, she left Manos and his parents at the hospital and flew to meet the producer in Los Angeles, at his invitation.

A year after the meeting with the television producer and once a contract had been signed, the series, 'Tempting maids', topped the rating charts for US series. Alexia Hudson-Sopholes had become a popular Hollywood star and the media flocked to her and her life story.

An interview broadcast from coast to coast by a leading national American network, on a 'night show' program entitled 'The maid who captivated Hollywood', was watched by ten million viewers. The sexy Greek film star was asked by the popular host: "What are your plans for the near future?" Alexia, the sexy Greek actor, promptly answered: "To act in a film with one of these two film stars... I have fantasized about them since I was little". She whispered the names of the two actors in the host's ear.

Less than a year later, Alexia Hudson Sopholes appeared in a movie with a famous Hollywood star, one of the two from her childhood fantasies, in a movie that became a great Hollywood blockbuster in two weeks: 'Fantasies come true'. Her name appeared in the promos beside that of the top star, the fantasy of her life.

Five years after she had first arrived from Athens at the hospital in

Philadelphia with Manos and his parents, Alexia Preston Sopholes was living happily in Hollywood with her husband, Mitt Preston, a successful film director, and their two year old son Manos.

Manos Neris, a decorated officer in the Greek artillery corps, adored young Manos, the son of Alexia and Mitt, his beloved nephew overseas. Over the years the wonderful connection between Manos the Greek and Manos the American and his parents grew and solidified, between Hollywood US and Athens, Greece ...

Never underestimate the 'simple and poor'. Even if their pockets are shallow, their hearts are big!

13

The law of the amazing numbers

● ● ●

Adam and Yaheli were happy twins, for several reasons. They had fun-loving and considerate parents, kind grandparents who gave them many presents, a cool great grandfather aged 101 with whom they had a wonderful relationship and shared love, simply a gift from heaven. Their's was a rare state of affairs compared to their close friends. They were well-loved and pleasant children. Their attractive comfortable home in Toronto, Canada, was located in a neighborhood with lots of gardens and overlooked a charming lake district. Their rooms were decorated with Disney themes and featured ample gadgets, loved by children their age. And they had other emotional and material reasons for their joie de vivre and youthful joy.

But all these pleasures were overshadowed with something they bore with them constantly, from the day they were born, not understanding why they had been encumbered by this 'burden'. Although they were popular, this 'bothersome thing' that followed them at all times aroused at times giggles and even derision among some of their friends. Occasionally the twins would be tormented due to this 'strange phenomenon'.

For seven or six years since they began the first grade they had been bothered by this issue that became even more irksome in time, as they approached adolescence. The two would be celebrating their 13th birthday in two months.

The charming twins would so like to leave this 'affliction' behind. They had never felt any connection to it and did not understand how and why it existed.

What afflicted and bothered them was no other than their surname: Numbers. They loathed their name. For several years they had asked their parents, Tammy and Irwin, to explain the source of their surname, which was a mental burden to them everywhere: at school, in the neighborhood, at extracurricular activities, and wherever they were asked for their full name. Their parents always referred them to Grandpa Ashley, their paternal grandfather, to solve the mystery of their name.

When they asked Grandpa Ashley, he, together with Grandma Betty, send them to Great-grandfather Bernie, saying that "only he can tell you the reason for our name, and why it is so important and precious for our family".

They indeed went to old Grandpa Bernie and begged him to tell them… but their proud and clearheaded great-grandfather with his soft voice said: "Adam and Yaheli, my dearest great-grandchildren, not today, not this time. I promise to tell you some other time… we'll find the right opportunity". He would add: "Meanwhile believe me, my dears, you can be very proud of this name. It's important that you know that the story of your surname is intriguing and important for all generations of our family, and you too are already part of it."

This was the usual process, and for years the twin great-grandchildren continued to nag and to ask their great-grandfather for the story and he, upright in almost every respect, evaded them again and again, until…

Wednesday, December 12, 2012. After years of great-grandfather Bernie's procrastinations, he decided that this was a suitable special date to carry out what he had been promising them for years, to tell them the story of their surname, Numbers. He was not getting any younger… it's time to tell!

This was certainly the moment the great-grandchildren had anticipated. He invited them, and only them, to the Mexican restaurant Tiko Tako, their favorite. He arranged with their father, his grandson, that they would call him when they concluded their meeting at the restaurant, and he would come and take all three of them home.

Around a small round table with a lantern on the checked cloth the great-grandfather launched into the incredible story of the origins of their surname. The twin great-grandchildren with their special charm had waited enthusiastically and eagerly for so long to hear this mysterious story…

"I will tell and you, my dearest beloved great-grandchildren, can ask me whatever you'd like…". Tears of joy once again coursed down the cheeks of this amazing man, 101 years and one month old. He was blessed to be at a restaurant with his loving great-grandchildren, in good health and at a ripe old age. Bernie told himself how lucky he was to have had such a rare and wonderful life.

"It all began with my father Boris who lived in Russia with my mother, Lydia. They were your great-great-grandfather and your great-great-grandmother, who died many years before you were born, my dearest great-grandchildren…

Your great-great-grandfather, my father, always loved to play with numbers, to construct all kinds of stories and legends with numbers, and it was important for him that family birthdays or events occurred on special numerical combinations.

My birth certificate and identification card show that I was born on a special date in the previous century, on the 11th day of the 11th month, nineteen eleven. It must have happened, and I've seen it often in writing, 11.11.11. My great-great-grandfather was happy to see this number associated with him and with our family.

Immediately after I was born, and by then we were living in Canada, in the city of Ottawa, where we had arrived from Russia, my father felt that he would like his name to sound more American or Canadian, rather than Russian. For this purpose he changed our surname from Sapisov to Numbers. He chose this name, of course, thanks to his great outstanding love for numbers… Later, I and the next generations caught on to this love of numbers. I really hope, my dearest Adam and Yaheli, that after this evening you too will continue the family tradition…"

"Grandpa, what happened later, were there other stories with such special numbers?" asked Adam inquisitively.

"Oh, that's a long story about amazing numbers, of course there are many more, after all we're the Numbers family…

"This story of mine will continue a long time after you finish eating, and tonight you can have as many desserts and drinks as you'd like. Tomorrow you'll be on vacation… we can remain here until late at night".

"That's great, great-grandfather Bernie, you're cool," Yaheli burst out happily. She was so happy to have been given an unexpected day of vacation.

"The next important date in our family is February 22, 1922..." continued the 101-year-old. As all his acquaintances knew, that was only one of his virtues...
"What happened then, great-grandfather?" asked Adam.
"On that day in the previous century we moved to Toronto from Ottawa, great-great-grandfather Boris with great-great-grandmother Lydia. He, of course, chose to move on a date marked by special numbers. Since we had the good luck to move to Toronto our lives improved immeasurably..."

The next important date that great-great-grandfather admired was 3.3.33. Three three three three...
"And what happened on that date, dear great-grandfather?" Adam asked in suspense.
"Several years before that date, beginning from 1929, American citizens had been suffering from financial problems. This had a bad effect on us in Canada as well, because we are America's neighbor. That period in the United States was called the Depression. Many people there lost their jobs, and even most of their money and possessions. It was a sad and bad time for us as well, although we lived in Canada and not in the United States, where things were even worse. By the time the Depression ended I was a young man of about 21. Great-great-grandfather, my father, said to me, 'Bernie my son, this is our opportunity to hit it big. After the Depression people will want to buy jewelry to cheer themselves up and to compensate themselves for the bad times they've been through. I know where to buy cheap jewelry. I'll open a shop and you'll learn from my Russian friend, the jeweler Sergei Paulov, how to make jewelry'... And that's how your great-great-grandfather, my father, opened the new shop in Toronto on..."
And his two great-grandchildren answered in unison, as though planned in advance: "On three three three three, our dear great-grandfather"
"True, true, my dearest, you are smart children. The smartest..."

Adam took Bernie to the restroom, giving the great-grandfather and his twin great-grandchildren an opportunity to take a break from the fascinating number story that was taking quite a while to tell.

Bernie and Adam returned from the restroom arm in arm. Yaheli received a kiss on the forehead and a pat from the amazing man on her long light-colored hair.

"And now guess what happened on 4.4.44, four four four four..." and he answered: "Your grandfather, Grandpa Ashley, was born exactly on that date. You must have learned in your history lessons that it was during World War II, and that America too joined this war towards the end".

"And what happened, grandpa, on five five five five?" Yaheli, the gifted great-grandaughter, could not restrain herself.
"Oh, that one I've forgotten, I'll have to check my diary at home..."

"And you, my dearest great-grandchildren, must want to know what happened on..." he quickly tried to smooth over the previous detail that he had forgotten.
The two continued in tandem: "On six six six six", they said in a rhythm they had just improvised. And then they said something else that made grandpa laugh with joy: "Six six six six, what a fix."
"That's an interesting story... on that day Grandpa Ashley graduated from university. Great-grandmother Olga and myself attended the event and we were very excited. We were very proud of him. The university liked that special date too... Six six six six, what a fix... The special date of the graduation ceremony shows that the university learned something from the Numbers family," he said and winked at his great-grandchildren...
The 101-year-old smiled joyfully when he said with pleasure that the university had 'learned' from his family. It also helped him hide his previous untypical lapse.

"Great-grandpa, we know what happened on seven seven seven seven", yelled the two in unison, continuing the story, which had suddenly become a fun and fascinating game.
"So you tell me..."

"Daddy Irwin was born on that date. He always says so proudly", Yaheli was the first to answer.
Adam added: "Great-grandpa Bernie, do you know what daddy told mommy Tammy on his birthday this year? I heard him tell her that he if had managed to get 'seven seven seven seven' on the casino slot machines, like the date of his birthday, we would have had lots of money."

Yaheli continued her twin brother's words and said: "That's right, I heard him too…"

"And great-grandpa, please go on telling us about eight eight eight eight. What happened in the Numbers family then?!" the great-granddaughter asked him to continue the mesmerizing story.

"Do you know that the number eight is considered the most important number in China?"

"Yes", Adam jumped up and said: "Our teacher Meryl told us about it in class. I remember that she told us that the Olympics in China began on eight eight eight eight…

Yaheli interrupted him and showed (again) incredible proficiency: "And at exactly eight and eight minutes."

"I always knew that my great-grandchildren were not only charming but also geniuses…" and he continued:

"And on that special date, the first day of the Olympics, your father's father, Grandpa Ashley, opened his successful jewelry manufacturing firm in China. He was one of the first Canadians to open a company in China with Chinese partners. And thank God, the company, belonging to your grandpa and your parents, has done very well over the years."

The energetic indefatigable old man drained his third or fourth glass of whiskey that night, followed by several spicy tacos.

"We know that on nine nine nine nine mommy and daddy, who were students, got married…" Yaheli interrupted him, once again demonstrating her knowledge of family events.

"Now you probably understand why your daddy chose that date to marry your mommy Tammy, although they were quite young at the time."

Their great-grandfather further told them that "On ten ten ten Toronto's social foundation, encouraging the nurturing of humane values, awarded the family badge of honor to myself and to the entire family as an example of family excellence, citing the heads of the prestigious foundation. We scored ten three times: for values, for heritage and tradition, and of course for our rare family relationship".

More than 88 years separated great-grandfather Bernie and his great-grandchildren, Adam and Yaheli. Judging by the enthusiasm aroused by the delights of this electrifying evening, the considerable age difference was not evident. All three were drawn by the incredible family numbers story, as though they were the same age…

"On 11.11.11, my 100th(!) birthday, your little sister Donna was born, my third great-grandchild whom we love so much…"
"When Donna is older and she can talk and understand, we will tell her this amazing story of the Numbers family together. Won't we, great-grandfather?!" Adam interrupted him
"I think you will tell her, I'll be old by then…"
"No, great-grandfather, you always stay young", the twins piped up in protest.
"We see, great-grandfather, that you are a little tired, so only one more question. Why were we born on a regular date, February 22, 2000?" asked Yaheli.
"I'm really very tired, please ask your father to come and take us home. I think it would be a good idea for him to come at 10, 10 minutes, and 10 seconds…"
"And I'm sure you remember, dear great-grandpa, that today is 12.12.12." said Adam.
"That's why great-grandpa asked to tell us the story today," Yaheli jumped in again.
"Wow, Yaheli, you've shown once again that you're smarter than me, but I'm more handsome than you."
"You're both the smartest and the prettiest in the world. And your sister Donna, of course."

The next day Yaheli and Adam visited their great-grandfather's private unit in their house. All night long both could not fall asleep in their rooms due to, or in fact thanks to, their incredible evening together. And today they had a special vacation.
They said to him: "We apologize, dear great-grandpa. We realized last night that the date we were born is not 'just another date', like we thought last night at the restaurant."
"Really? What did you find out?"
"That mommy and daddy planned this cool date for us…"
"What do you mean, my dearest great-grandchildren?"
"We're sure you know, you're just pulling our leg… On the cool date of February 22, 2022 we will both be 22!"
"You are two geniuses, my two lovelies, two charming, two incredible."
They didn't tell great-grandpa which of them had made the discovery

that amazed him, their great-grandfather, a discovery that he himself had calculated on the day they were born, when he became a great-grandfather and his wife Olga a great-grandmother. He didn't really care who it was. For him, both his 'loves' had found out together. The two great-grandchildren promised him that they would continue the family dynasty, the special dates, marking special days in their own lives and those of the following generations… They would do everything to make this happen.

101-year-old Bernie was incredibly happy. The lengthy tradition and heritage of the amazing numbers of the Numbers dynasty was guaranteed for the next generations as well.

To the regret of his dearest great-grandchildren, great-grandpa Bernie did not reach their 22nd birthday party on February 22, 2022… but the family heritage continues.

The more global the world, the more efforts should be made to strengthen family heritage; any time, in any way.

14

The Englishwoman who remained for an entire trip on the tube

● ● ●

Until that evening, arrogant Pierre was convinced that French girls and women were the best. He was certain of this due to their fastidious appearance, their femininity, and above all their sexuality. To all these he probably added his rich experience with them. Pierre, a tall man at one meter ninety, was the very epitome of the endeavor to 'seek the woman', maybe the most famous French cliché. And he did not stop at seeking. He almost always found her. He always hit it off with the opposite sex.

That special weekend he decided to cross the channel and forego another adventure in the City of Lights in favor of his second big love: soccer. Since scoring and kicking French soccer stars had recently been opting to join British teams, French fans had also gradually begun traveling to London soccer fields to watch their idols, players who chose to play for the country that had always been an avowed rival of the French. Times had changed, young people had become more global and less local patriots. And so Pierre as well found himself a fan of London-based Arsenal, favoring that team over his childhood favorite, Paris St. Germain. True, in a sense it felt like betrayal. But his many interchanging romantic affairs had left him immune to betrayal. A major game in the top

British league had brought Pierre to London that weekend. He managed to combine a visit to a good English friend, who lived in the posh area of Hampstead Heath. He was staying there, sparing himself the need to search for a suitable hotel during London's tourist-filled Easter holidays. It was a winning combination of a soccer game, the vibrant city, and visiting a friend. He had been an Arsenal fan for the past two years thanks to its 5-6 (!) players from France and its overseas colonies who aroused the pride of all French soccer fans. Some of the French players, mostly the dark-skinned, had a regular place on the starting lineup. And all thanks to the French coach who made sure that the team was 'half French' as it was called by the British media, who were not happy with this state of affairs, which angered many British soccer fans. For French soccer fans, however, this was one way to make fun of Britain in general and of British soccer in particular.

His British friend James, whom he had met when they were both studying business management, was hosting Pierre at his home. He invited him to come to a party at the home of his friend Penny nearby. Pierre agreed, but he sounded reserved, unenthusiastic. He was skeptical of the female allure of English women. He considered them inhibited and dull. True, he was aware of his bias, and that he was a prisoner of his own stigmas. In this context he always liked to cite a stereotypical poem that he had learned and that sometimes helped him avoid dangerous images. He felt that the poem did not give credit to French men for being excellent lovers. So before refusing his friend's offer he asked himself, 'Maybe I'm wrong about the image of British women?' and thus, in a moment of stereotypical confession, on the way to the improvised party at James' friend's, he recited the following piece for his friend:

"What is a European Paradise?
A place that has…
British cops
French cooks
German mechanics
Italian lovers
And everything is organized by the Swiss…

What is a European Hell?
A place that has…
British cooks

French mechanics
Swiss lovers
German cops
And everything is organized by the Italians…"
"And it galls me," said Pierre to his British friend, that "the Italians, the little scoundrels, are considered the best lovers while we only get credit for our cooking – what a distorted view."
"Yes," nodded his friend James, "I too am annoyed that our women attract such derision for being pale females and uninterested sexual partners… although as you know I have no real interest in the female sex. I'm glad you're ready to change your views. I remember how I changed my views on French management when I came to France to study and we met."

When they rang the bell and the pink door with the blue butterfly opened, admitting them to the house in the alley, Pierre felt upon glimpsing the living room that maybe this time he was wrong. Like the mistake with the 'European heaven'… Eight women aged 25-30 sat in a circle and at first glance showed nothing of the typical British female aloofness, at least judging by their daring attire. And definitely by the 'ravaging' gazes of half of those present who stared at the two men. After James hugged Penny, their host, and the French guest was introduced and shook her hand, they entered the living room.

The captivating Frenchman realized from the first few minutes that he would have a tough choice. The mantra within him received an addition of one word: 'right', namely 'search for the right woman'. The impressive selection of women was almost his for the picking: James was a declared homosexual, and the two other men were bent over an i-pad and deep in conversation, their eyes glued to the small screen. The evening progressed, with unlimited drinks and giggles, including some jokes combining French and English. The two men with the i-pad showed no special interest in the women, and only joined in in the fun from time to time. The Frenchman quickly became the 'king of the women's circle'. He managed to communicate excellently with the thirsty women. And they were not thirsty only for wine, beer, or other alcohol. It was great fun but all in all pretty vacuous. The women listened to tales of life at the Sorbonne in Paris and of the wonderful friendship between Pierre the womanizer and gay James. At this stage these were the most interesting moments in the party.
Pierre told them about opening his software business for virtual marketing.

He said that he is now seeking to develop and market a product that would delight women all over the world and make him rich. He plans to buy two homes, one in Montparnasse, Paris, and the other in Hampstead Heath, London, so that he can frequently come and visit this group with which he is having such a good time. In the midst of all the drinking and fooling around, he suddenly remarked that virtual arousal is the best. He immediately realized that this statement left him in the minority among the eight women and four men at the improvised party. Most said that there's nothing like the frustration of 'virtual reality'. Pierre did not give up and attempted to prove that suspense and imagination are more stimulating than the grey reality, in his words.

Penny, the energetic red-haired host, cut into Pierre's tomfoolery. Surprisingly, she invited all her women friends to leave the living room and come into the kitchen with her. There she asked for their cooperation in preparing a surprise for 'our good looking guest from France'. They returned after 3 minutes of creative thinking…

Penny turned down the Spice Girls music in the background. For the first time in the last hour she put down the glass of gin she had been holding. Then she yelled, rousing both floors of the magnificent house, half roaring and half giggling, wiggling her sexy behind: "Pierre, you are undoubtedly the star of the evening; excuse me, the star of the night! We all think that you have earned a bonus from the women here. Choose one of us. Whomever you'd like, but know that one, only one of us can be with you for your entire four day visit to our city… although tonight you will not be able to enjoy her company. Then again, none of the other seven will be with you throughout your visit. But any one of them can spend this night with you. Only one. You can choose one and be with her…"

Pierre the Frenchman and James the Englishman were equally astounded.

Penny continued passionately: "And that one of us, the ultimate escort, will be at her best behavior every moment of your visit here, aside from tonight. Your chance of choosing her is 1 in 8. Everyone happily agreed to this 'deal' in the kitchen.

By the way, the only one of us who is married, and you don't know who she is, is also the only one who if chosen will be with you throughout your visit aside from tonight. And this escort service has good reason. From here on it's your choice, but it's also your gamble. By the way, we hope that you will no longer attach to British women the stigma of being cold and unfeminine, as you told your friend. We will no longer agree to be put down by French men!"

James and Pierre were still shocked by the surprise and by the tempting offer. And in general, by everything that had occurred and been said over the past few minutes. The gay Englishman decided to shut up and stuffed his mouth with a fat sausage.

"I love the TV program 'Millionaire' and since I have three candidates that are to my liking, I am attracted to each of the three, and my fantasy is that the one I choose will indeed be with me throughout my stay in London. I believe that I will be able to tempt her to forget the rules and spend the night with me as well. I need a hint." said Pierre, who felt that the evening was 'right down his alley'…"

Once again Penny summoned the other seven women into the kitchen and all eight left, giving their hint in unison: "The woman in question loves the London tube, and the more you travel on the underground, the tube, the more you'll enjoy her, from every angle, and certainly her wonderful gaze…"

"Can I begin by choosing 4 women and then you, Penny, will tell me if the chosen one is one of the four: Debbie, Nora, Shandy, or Penny?!"

"Yes!" answered all the women, half of whom had reached the 'semi finals' while the other half had been rejected by the single judge. Pierre felt encouraged, knowing that the one and only 'escort' was one of those he had named.

'The escort' was the name given by James to the rapidly evolving game. It was also a sign that he had managed to overcome his shock at the game. "Too bad," he muttered to himself, "that I don't have eight male partners to play the same cool game with me…"

Pierre asked permission to write down his choice on a note that he would give to James. This was a way of not embarrassing himself or the women who awaited his decision. James was an objective observer, while Penny, who had reached the 'semi finals', had a stake in the results. He handed the note to his friend and not to his red-haired host, who was delighted with the creative game she had devised. Nonetheless, she was on edge, waiting to see whether it would be her night.

The tension in the room increased. Even the two men with the i-pad were showing interest in the results…

Pierre chose the sensual brunette Shandy, who seemed to him the most liberal. From the beginning of the evening she had been his choice, but he hadn't let on, so that all the others would continue to vie for his attention. He loved being courted… Penny opened the repeatedly folded note. She nodded and roared in laughter, rousing the entire neighborhood: "S-h-a-

n-d-y, S-h-a-n-d-y…"
Everyone clapped and roared "Pierre Pierre, Shandy Shandy!"

Pierre and Shandy climbed the stairs to the second floor and remained on their own in Penny's romantic bedroom with the canopy bed. It was an impressive room with sculptures and folklorist artwork from all over Africa. Pierre did not get his night of passion with the woman of his choice.
But once they were in the bedroom Shandy quickly gave him her telephone number and told him that it was late and she had to go home. She reminded him that she was the only married woman and the only one, according to the 'rules', who had not promised to sleep with him. But the next morning, at 11am, he could see her near the main ticket booth, at the Hampstead tube station, on the platform of the Black Northern line to Baker Street. From then on she would be with him in many beautiful places all over London, the city that had welcomed him into its midst this evening. She would be his escort. And winking at him she laid her hand on his neck and promised that he would have lots of virtual pleasures to enjoy just as he liked, at least according to his stories tonight.

Pierre did not 'score a goal' that night. He hoped he would the next day, and that his Arsenal would win the championship too.

Pierre couldn't fall asleep that night at the home of his friend James. He counted the few remaining hours until his designated encounter with Shandy. His passion for her and for the adventures that awaited him over the next few days only grew in his heart, in his mind, and in another sensitive part of his body. They would be together for four fascinating days, minus some time for soccer with Arsenal. Shandy would change his perception of British women.

10:45 He arrived early at the Hampstead tube station and stood at the place they had agreed upon next to the ticket booth.
11:00 Shandy had still not arrived. All types of women passed through the ticket both on their way to the tube, but not Shandy.
11:05 Shandy did not answer the mobile phone number that she had given him.
11:30 Pierre left the ticket booth and searched the platform for the train heading for Baker Street.
To his bitter disappointment, Shandy was not there. But then, to his amazement, she was indeed there virtually. Shandy looked out at him

from everywhere, from her place in the impressive poster advertising the airport's duty free shops. And from station to station Pierre became all the more enamored of Shandy. Suddenly he realized that real is always better than virtual. He felt that he had erred twice the night before, and once he had also made a bad gamble. It was too much for him. He was also aware of the trick that the eight women had played on him in the kitchen. He felt the sweet revenge for his stigma of British women as unfeminine and cold. Even on the eighth try, Shandy did not answer the telephone number she had given him the night before.

Shandy 'was with him' all the way to Arsenal's Emirates stadium in northwest London. She appeared on all platforms of the stations for the markets he loved to visit on the tube – trendy Camden Market, Portobello Market in Nottingham Hill with its antiques, and the old Petticoat Lane market on Liverpool Street. Everywhere, even on the way to the airport, Shandy featured sensuously in illuminated signs. And the more he saw her in the posters, the more he felt that she was meant to teach him a lesson about life, but at the same time also inspire him to achieve an outstanding commercial success.

Once again he appraised Shandy's posters, with her million pound look that enveloped him virtually. The beautiful woman from the party and in the posters encouraged viewers to buy at London's duty free shops, under the advertising slogan: 'Duty Free: set yourself for the flight.'

Having seen many of these posters, once he reached the airport he suddenly realized the meaning of the word 'set', used in the ad in association with flying. The word 'set', which meant 'ready' in the ad, now received another meaning for him. He had an inspiration that millions of women would wish to buy a set of accessories that would give them a good feeling, consisting of (almost) everything they needed on a plane, a winning brand name set called "Lady Set on Jet".

Three and a half years after that unforgettable weekend, Pierre had become a marketing tycoon. He purchased a beautiful ancient house in the most exclusive part of Hampstead Heath, London. Another home faced his favorite café in Montparnasse, Paris. He also decided to buy another house in Shanghai, China, to be close to the factory manufacturing the product he had begun marketing two and a half years earlier, inspired by Shandy: a kit that included skin care, beauty, and makeup products, perfumed wipes, and a small pad of paper with a miniature pen, under the brand name Lady Set on Jet.

The large factory in China with its 1200 employees could not keep up with demands for the popular kit at duty free shops in European and American countries.

Pierre knew that he owed his fortune to the publicity campaign led by Shandy who had 'stood him up' at the Hampstead tube station in London but appeared repeatedly in all her British allure in all other stations of the tube.

He would never forget the spring weekend that had changed his rigid stereotype of English women and turned him into a business tycoon in the promising triangle of: Paris-Shanghai-London... From time to time he remembers to thank sensuous Shandy..

Stigmas and stereotypes are the enemies of progress and creativity. Leaving them behind is essential.

15

The Halils and the Galils – Two couples meet in Copenhagen

● ● ●

In those early morning moments in Copenhagen's harbor the 'mermaid' seemed even smaller than she actually was. In reality this famous sculpture, perched on a rock, appears smaller than imagined by tourists. Millions of fantasizing visitors come to Copenhagen to see for themselves the beauty and power of this eternal icon. In posters, photographs, travel guides, websites, and even in collective imagination, the sculpture seems like a large impressive and powerful monument. But in fact it is not so, to the disappointment of many who come to see the sculpture, inspired by Hans Christian Andersen's enchanting tale 'The Mermaid', written in 1836. He himself was a legend in his lifetime.

The gloomy weather in the early hours of this day in mid-August increased the disappointment of the few visitors who had ventured out early to view the sculpture. Their sense of frustration stemmed from the disparity between their imagination and the reality of the famous mermaid's dimensions. As the story goes, the mythological young girl surpassed all her four sisters and was the favorite of her father, king of the sea.
The waves crashed on the rock holding the fabled sculpture, and the

fantasies of many of the visitors usually disappeared with the waves, be they stormy or not.

The clashing of imagination and reality formed a main element in the exciting and fascinating encounter that proceeded to take place on that outstanding morning at the harbor, opposite the famous mermaid. Who knows, maybe the unusual incident was in fact inspired by her…?!

It all began when an Israeli couple standing at the harbor approached a dark-complexioned couple who despite their Arabic accent were speaking an unidentified Scandinavian language. This couple, with their Arab countenance, were the only people standing near the two Israelis at that moment in the early hours at Denmark's pleasant lively capital, the capital of a hardworking and sympathetic country beloved by many.
At that constitutive moment, which subsequently generated a fantastic, some may say historical development, the middle aged Israeli man asked the man beside him in polite English whether he would be willing to photograph him and his wife with the mermaid. The pleasant young man, wearing an elegant suit, flashed a smile that showed all his white teeth and was happy to comply. He even seemed enthusiastic, taking two other pictures from different angles at the request of the Israeli. In the process, he thought to himself about the significance of one's viewpoints and outlook on life. This was in fact an important motto in his life.

At this time, organized tour groups who had arrived on site at that early hour in two tourist buses, one German and the other French, as well as several independent visitors who had come by themselves, were all at the harbor, facing the mermaid, a total of about 70-80 tourists. The two couples – the Israeli and the Arab – were conspicuous. The Israelis stood out because of the age difference between the man and the woman, who appeared to be at least two decades apart. Their passion, manifested by fervent kisses and constant caresses, left no doubt that these were not a father and his daughter.
The second couple, with their Arab appearance, formed a confusing impression. The woman wore a veil but removed it from time to time and then covered her face again, and this happened repeatedly over a short span of time. This act aroused special interest among the visitors. When the young woman's face was exposed her beauty was evident. She herself could not decide which state was best, with or without the veil. She was clearly undecided. The elegant Lamborghini parked near

them, which the dark-skinned man approached to retrieve a bag, was also not entirely compatible with the veiled image of his partner.

The two couples represented different cultures, different religions – and were to a great degree opposites. The two women had their attractive beauty in common, although each was different: the dark tone and aquamarine eyes versus the blonde with the blue eyes, the hesitating versus the smiling face. The two couples could not have imagined the results of their random meeting and the incredible events that would consequently befall them.
Other elements divided the two couples from the rest of the tourists at that point in time, aside from their appearance. Ultimately, it was a hidden difference, maybe even a mystical one, associated with something much deeper, more fundamental, a difference connected to their reasons for coming to see the sculpture at the harbor for the first time. For both couples it was not simply another tourist site as it was for all the others and for the millions of tourists who had been there before them, throughout the decades since the installation of the mermaid sculpture in Copenhagen.

The planned visit of each of the couples to the sculpture of the mermaid had a moving and meaningful purpose; different for each, but as we will see, also similar. Each of the two purposes was enveloped in lots of appeal and nostalgia. For each couple the visit held a great deal of significance for their relationship.

Leila and Mousa had made the trip from northern Sweden, where they lived, to the site of the sculpture. The man appeared to be in his late twenties; the woman, when her face was revealed, seemed in her mid-twenties.
The two had driven their magnificent car from the charming coastal town of Lulea, in northern Sweden. The reason for their visit here was a combination of a wish come true and a revelation of their family story. Mousa had vowed that once his wife Leila would be with child, carrying a male baby, he would bring her here to show her where and how his roots began. Here in this place his parents had met, prominent Lebanese refugees who fled Lebanon after many days of terrible fighting between Christians and Muslims in the divided land of the cypresses. As property-owning refugees, Mousa's parents and their families had been given the option of living in Scandinavia. His mother had lived with her family in Copenhagen before meeting his father and his father had lived with his

family in Guttenberg, Sweden, with a holiday home in Lulea. They were both students – he in Stockholm and she in Copenhagen. They first met at a gathering of Arab students, opposite the sculpture to which their son had now returned. His father had told him this story of how they had met, and he had come for the first time to make true his promise and tell the story to his beloved wife Leila.

During the three years of their marriage Mousa had told Leila many times that his Lebanese father and mother had met at a special place and in special circumstances. He had promised to take her there and tell her the story when it became clear that she was carrying a male descendant. That would be the news he was hoping for, to continue his parents' lineage.

Mousa also told her repeatedly that on that occasion 'in that special place', in his words, he would tell her a fascinating family story related to his parents, one that was the most influential event in his life and in that of Leila herself. He couldn't have been more dramatic.

And now, only a few minutes ago, he had told her: "Everything began here. This is where my mother and father first met. They were the son and daughter of affluent families who left Lebanon following the ethnic and religious civil war. My parents met here. They fell in love at first sight. They married and had a family. In time, my two young brothers went to visit relatives in Tripoli, Lebanon. One was 18 years old and the other 16. They were both killed in a terror attack and I remained my parents' only living son".

Leila had been waiting eagerly for three years to hear the promised story at the promised place. She was no different than most other women in this respect. She was anxious to hear the story of her beloved husband, the man she admired who was rich in three respects: First, in money and property. As the only living son of his parents he was the only heir to the large fortune of his parents, among the richest people in Guttenberg, Sweden's second largest city. They and their son Mousa were known for their wealth. Second, her man was rich in stories and parables. Some he had heard from his father, some he had read, and others – quite a few – he had composed himself and then told others. Third, her beloved was rich in generosity. He gave generously to the needy and invested large sums in a foundation that developed humanitarian projects, mainly for children and the young.

Leila knew that her husband was very fond of seeing her beautiful face. But she also respected her Muslim upbringing. Her parents had asked, rather than demanded, that she wear a veil. Of all five sisters she was her parents' favorite. Just like the mermaid, who of all five daughters of the king of the sea was his favorite. At a certain moment at the harbor, when she heard the story of the mermaid, she thought that maybe Mousa had in mind this similarity between the five daughters. I am the favorite versus the favorite mermaid. And she knew that her husband had a good imagination. She loved his wild imagination. She was also in love with that imagination, which she considered a gift of God to her husband.

The passion shown by Mousa the husband, the educated man, for her beauty contrasted with her need to respect her parents' wishes, often creating a conflict for Leila: passion versus tradition, the beloved husband versus the loving parents, and also her thoughts versus her feelings. So she alternated her use of the veil. Sometimes when she was outside she felt that the veil was evil, and sometimes she felt that it was of avail.

Leila was different than her sisters. She was liberal, open to other religions and cultures, a 'hardcore' internet fan. She also had strong opinions on current affairs, which normally occupied only the men in her society. Even the championship soccer games of the Barcelona team fascinated her... When the Israeli asked her husband to photograph him and his wife, she felt a little insulted – why hadn't he addressed both of them, she said to herself. She can photograph just as well, and when he had turned to them she had not been wearing her veil.

Leila's intuition was almost always right, and it had helped her out in many situations. Even in an arranged marriage proposed before she met Mousa, when she was introduced to a tall handsome man, a Lebanese scientist who came all the way to Sweden from Venezuela to meet her, as part of a complex family plan to connect two parts of the family, in Caracas and Malma. She refused the match adamantly and would not see the man again after their initial introduction at her house in the presence of her parents and two of her sisters. As a result of this rejection, she even became estranged from her family for a short while. In time it became clear that her intuition had (once again) been correct. The scientist, presented as an honorable man, eventually turned out to be a habitual woman beater and a professional charlatan. When very young, she had also refused matches with two other men. Mousa, she felt intuitively even before meeting him, would be the man of her life. This deep feeling was based only on stories she had heard of him. Several minutes after seeing him, when he arrived at her family home in Malma from Guttenberg, she already knew that she had not been mistaken. In the three years that they were together, despite the rigors of the fertility treatments, she realized how right she had been. Mousa was an angel sent to her from Allah to carry her aloft.

Today's visit to Copenhagen's mermaid by the Swedish couple of Lebanese descent was a way of reaching closure on several important issues in their life: Leila's desire to satisfy Mousa, the success of her fertility treatments in the form of the first trimester of a pregnancy with a male embryo, and her noble husband's promise to tell her his story, which he called 'It all began here!'.

* * *

When Moshe, the good-looking middle aged Israeli, asked Mousa to photograph him and his wife, Leila was still very excited by the secret Mousa had disclosed to her 10 minutes previously. He had told her the reason for their journey from the holiday town in Sweden to the mermaid in Denmark. She was still under the impact of the story, related after three years of increasing intrigue.

Ronit, in contrast, was still in the 'pre' stage. She was still waiting eagerly to hear the resolution of the mystery, Moshe's revealing of a dramatic life story, why he had brought her to Copenhagen… What does this place have to do with his being an author, now a successful one, and most amazing, he had never been to Copenhagen. So how was it possible that this place had had such an effect on his life? Until last night, when she arrived at the airport, Ronit had not known where they were headed. Moshe had kept it a complete secret, as though part of the beginning of a new mysterious novel he was writing. The unsolved riddle had only intensified when she heard last night where they were going. "Why Copenhagen, what is the connection to his success?" She only knew that in Copenhagen, where they were headed, he would tell her the secret of the story, or rather, the story of the secret that had brought them there. She was convinced that she had no chance of extracting the story from him on the flight. Their destination was only revealed to her during the security check at Ben Gurion Airport.

They had been at the harbor in Copenhagen, next to the sculpture, for only 15 minutes before her husband asked the courteous man to take their picture. She let her husband take his time. She had been waiting very patiently for the promised story for several years, not to mention on the plane. So she would remain patient for several more minutes. It couldn't take much longer.

Moshe had been an average author of mediocre novels that aroused no enthusiasm in the book stores. None of his first five books was featured on the bestseller lists. Each title sold several thousand copies in one or two editions. This was true of his first 18 years as an author, a career that was barely enough to make a living. He supplemented his income by working as a news editor at a local radio station. He seemed to be better at this than at writing.

About four years ago, his personal and professional life was dramatically transformed. One consequence was that amazing lively Ronit was now here with him, with the honorable title of his 'young wife and love of his life', in his words.
Ronit read one of his books, 'I'm not myself' (the only one that had had some success at the time), and fell in love with the author. She obtained his telephone number, contacted him, and impressed him with her female and artistic skills. He was spellbound by the fact that she was willing to leave her fiancé to marry him, Moshe, despite their large age difference. Almost every day since they had met was full of endless and mutual passion and love, which only increased over time.

Four months ago, Moshe Galil published his eighth book inspired by her (after the sixth and seventh books too had received lukewarm reviews and mediocre sales). The new novel, inspired by his relationship with Ronit, 'Love is everything', became a hysterical bestseller in one month. Otherwise they would not have been here now.
Throughout his years as an author he had vowed to himself that when one of his books gained a place on the bestseller lists he would tell his story to the woman who was his loving partner at the time, and also tell her to whom he owes his well-developed imagination and in what circumstances. Copenhagen would be the best place to reveal this, and the local complex with the mermaid sculpture would be the ideal location to reveal his secret.
Moshe had fantasized about Denmark since he was 'born' in Copenhagen, a city he had never set eyes on until this morning, when they landed here in an overnight flight in the spacious business class. They had rushed here from the airport in their rental car, without even checking in at the classy hotel where he had reserved a spacious suite overlooking large parts of the city.

Since he and Ronit had been together he had promised her, in a mantra that repeated itself weekly: "One day I will tell you where the seeds of my excessive imagination were sown and grew. I will do so in an appropriate place, thanks to the wonderful association of this monumental site with my imagination... The story might make you fall into the water around the site... and as an artist you will also see a famous piece of artwork there..."

"When will it be?!" Ronit asked him repeatedly. She was an impressive artist who had left her millionaire diamond merchant fiancé for the not-so-successful author when the latter dazzled her with his book (later on she read the others as well). From that first reading she aimed to reach his body and then managed, with her female and other skills, to enter his heart as well. There was something in his books, despite their mediocrity, that linked her to him. She believed in his ability to lift off as a successful author.

When asked 'When will he take her and tell her?' he answered in all sincerity, although sounding strange and illogical: "When I see a new book of mine on the bestseller list. It will probably happen while you are still a sexy woman with the joy of youth, and I will remain in full vigor with you forever..."

And now, not strange and not illogical. They were here. The bestselling author, at his advanced age, and the fairly young and beautiful artist, had reached the moment when he would tell his wife the secret as promised.

In these moments Moshe felt that the mermaid was far from the glory and power he had imagined, fantasizing about her since his childhood and 'birth' in Denmark, since he had first been exposed to the tales of Hans Christian Andersen, which had fascinated him. For so many years he had longed to be here. And now the two conditions had been fulfilled:

The first, his book 'Love is everything' has been on the bestseller lists since its publication, and had already been rapidly translated into English, thanks to the enthusiasm of the American publisher who bought the translation rights, and the book would be published in the US in about a month. The first English copy, printed on a home printer, was in his suitcase in their rental car.

The second condition: He now has a suitable wife whom he can tell 'how and where it all began...'.

Both conditions had been fulfilled – and they were here. They are here.

He had postponed the trip for three months to enjoy the fruit of his success, including many interviews in the media, and successfully managed negotiations with his publisher to sell the translation and distribution rights to his book in more than 10 countries, among them the United States, as mentioned.

The Arab couple had aroused Moshe's curiosity from the moment he and Ronit had reached the harbor. He had fought against the Arabs in three wars. The two near them seemed to him a pleasant Arab couple. Something deep within him urged him to try and start a conversation with them. Ronit had a similar feeling. Moshe found a good excuse to address the man and asked him to photograph them. Their contact was no less important than the photographs, maybe even more so. After he and Ronit had been photographed he offered to do the same for the other couple. They thanked him, smiling, and when the pictures had been taken he felt that they were open for conversation.

Moshe addressed them – this time turning to the woman too, as evident from his body language – and asked: "Are you having a good time here?" The polite Arab man answered, hinting that he wished to develop the conversation further: "We came here for a very special reason. Much more meaningful than seeing a nice sculpture… and what about you, have you found it interesting? Where are you from?"

Ronit and Moshe answered together in English: "We're from Israel, and it is indeed interesting and nice here…" And Ronit continued: "Despite the forbidding sky… and in addition, there is still a surprise in store for me," she said, drawing the two couples closer, attracted by the place and time, their willingness proving intuitively, or mystically, that they were destined to meet here and now.

"Ronit," Moshe addressed her in English in the presence of the other couple, in an attempt to further develop the spontaneous encounter, "Is it okay if I tell them why we're here?!"

Ronit knew that her husband Moshe would not stop at anything, and she was not surprised by his unusual suggestion.

"If they'd like to, of course, it's your story and it can be a joint experience for all of us, and maybe the inspiration for your next bestseller," she answered in English.

Mousa and Leila were totally amazed by their inclusion, by the rapid development, and by meeting a 'different type of Israeli' for the first time, at least when compared to the negative image they had received previously.

"We'd love to. It would be our honor," answered Mousa. "Do you mind that we are Lebanese in origin?!" he added, partly joking and partly serious. It was his way of revealing their country of origin.

"It will probably make our experience even more intense," answered Moshe.

"Thank you for the generous offer," Leila added, and immediately stuck the veil she had been holding into her bag. This time she felt at ease without it.

"Let's go into the café over there; it's a cold and overcast day, and so unexpected. We'll have something hot to drink. We seem so different from the other tourists…"

"Leila and I would be very glad to come and listen. We're in no hurry, and we both love stories. If Leila agrees I'll take my 'revenge' and tell you why we're here as well. We too have a very special story."

"I'm Moshe."

"And I'm Mousa."

"I'm Ronit."

"And I'm Leila."

Moshe said with a big smile: "It's a good thing Ronit isn't called Lily, otherwise it would have been very confusing: Mousa and Moshe, Leila and Lily."

"Who will go first?" Moshe was eager to tell his story to this larger but still intimate 'audience' and to reveal that he is a writer.

"The first to offer," answered Mousa who could not imagine any other option.

The four sat enthralled for two whole hours. Morning gave way to noon. The sun peeked out of the clouds for several minutes, in Nordic miserliness, and illuminated the joint experience of the four.

Moshe and Mousa were excellent storytellers, and their wives had always been fascinated by their incredible stories. The women served as wonderful ideal listeners for their husbands.

This time, however, in this unusual but intriguing situation, the husbands brought their stories to new and amazing heights, and their revelations as well. After all, that was why the two had brought their wives here from a distance.

Although Leila had heard the story from her husband only a short while ago, she was astonished once again, and her excitement did not reveal that she had already heard the story, after three years of anticipation that ended this morning with the magic that continued until the present with the Israeli couple.

Moshe said that it had all started in the third grade at a new school he joined when his family moved and he was 'uprooted', in his words, from his friends at the end of the second grade. He remembered word for word what his teacher Dina had said on the first day of school in his new classroom:

"We have three new students: the first is Moshe G., because we already have Moshe D. and Moshe K, and also Brurya and Ze'ev.

"Moshe G., welcome to the third grade. Where were you born?"

The teacher had welcomed him and asked him, decades ago.

"And then I surprised the teacher, the class, and myself more than all. Although I was born in Naharia, in Israel, I said confidently: 'I was born in Denmark!' From that moment the entire class idolized me. The teacher asked 'Where exactly?' and I answered: 'In Copenhagen'.

From age 4 and a half or 5 I remembered the fascinating stories my father Nachman had told me of how the Danish people had valiantly saved the Jews from the Nazis and their collaborators during the Holocaust. They were almost the only European nation to do so, my father told me. My father admired the Danish people, like many other Israelis who had similar feelings for the residents of Denmark.

My father's family was killed in the Holocaust in Hungary. At night, before I fell asleep, my father liked to tell me and my twin sister Galia the tales and stories of Hans Christian Andersen. We were both infatuated with the author and his stories. In time, when I learned to read, I enthusiastically read almost all his works. Today as an author I understand that the tales he wrote were suitable not only for children but also for adults and that was why my father loved this greatest of Denmark's authors. My father, with his imagination, had always remained a child."

You could cut the suspense with a knife. The three were fascinated and did not move, enthralled by the story that did not cease to surprise, and by the author who drew them along with his revelations.

"And each time the children asked me to tell them more about Denmark", Moshe continued, "I asked my father to tell me more stories about Denmark. And he told heroic tales of the Virtuous among the Nations, who risked their lives to save Jews during the Holocaust. He also fascinated us with his stories of the Danish Vikings, the Danish kings, their castles, and also about the Danish fishermen and the industrious Danish people, widening his scope to stories of all Scandinavia.

I told the stories, tales, experiences that had supposedly happened to me until age seven, to my classmates, and sometimes even to the teacher. I lied and said that at that age I had arrived in Israel, and then I improvised and said that 'from age seven to eight we lived on a kibbutz near Haifa, where I went to school for a year, and this summer we arrived in Naharia and at my new school here. From Denmark…'

I designed my stories to match the fact that I had lived in Denmark until I was seven, and gathered enough experiences and memories to tell my new classmates, in order to sound authentic. It was an incredible part of my life… This continued until I myself believed that I had really been born in Denmark…

And this is how I received the biggest present from my father whom I admired: a limitless literary imagination.

My father himself had dreamt of being an author, and I was the one to realize his dream. Until the day he died he was proud that I had chosen to be a writer. It's a pity that he himself did not live to see my last book, which I told him about before he closed his eyes for the last time…

And this morning, right after landing in Copenhagen, we drove here. Ronit is hearing this for the first time, my dearest, how and when my author's seeds of calamity and craziness were sowed."

Mousa and Leila were astonished and happy. Ronit, the love of Moshe's life, remained enthralled.

"That's it. That's my story," said Moshe. "Now it's your turn."

Ronit asked for a moment to go to their rental car, parked five minutes from the café. "I need a few minutes," she said and left excitedly.

Moshe took advantage of Ronit's departure and continued his conversation with Mousa and Leila:

"You must be curious about how we met, my wife and I, as we are clearly so far apart in age. 21 years, to be exact. This is a good time to tell you, with Ronit away:

Ronit wrote to me 4 years ago, a reader's letter that caught my attention. Atypically for me, I met with her. I fell in love, and a short while later we married in Cyprus in a civil marriage ceremony.

Four months ago I realized a dream. For the first time, one of my books attained the bestseller list in my country and it will soon be published in other countries as well. That's our special reason for being here today. I have fulfilled my promise to Ronit, given at our wedding, that if and when one of my books became a bestseller we would travel to the country that helped me become an author.

And here, dear Leila and Mousa, to our joy fate has brought us together, here with you… You are part of the intense experience of revealing the secret of how I became an author..."

The moment he finished the sentence Ronit appeared, carrying the single home printed copy of the book in English from their car, and said to Moshe: "Dedicate the first copy of your book in English to this charming couple".

All three were extremely surprised.

Leila recovered and when Ronit paused in excitement she said:

"Sign it only once Mousa has also told you why we're here."

Mousa thanked Leila and amazed everyone with the story that he had already told her. The fascinating mesmerizing experience was now related from the other side of the table, from the other culture.

It was the most amazing and enchanting day in the life of the four people who had arrived early that morning at the site of the Copenhagen mermaid. They could not have imagined to themselves in a million years, or even a billion, what would come of their exciting visit.

The Lebanese dinner the next day, at the incredibly beautiful villa several meters from the beach, in the high-class neighborhood of the town Lulea, was extremely moving and delicious. Mousa's parents and his brother Ibrahim hugged Moshe and Ronit warmly.

They all admired the book, and even more – its heartfelt dedication to Mousa and Leila, signed by Ronit and Moshe.

Two fruitful, wonderful years after the totally unconventional meeting of the four, Mousa Halil and Moshe Galil received an honorable award in Copenhagen entitled 'Humanitarian Success of the Year' from Paul Larsen, head of the prestigious Scandinavian organization, Humanitarianism Today, for their Scandinavian enterprise. The personally invited audience honored the winners with loud applause that went on and on.

The project was attended by 30 children, half Israeli Jews and half Palestinian Arabs.

The name of the enterprise was "ISLAEL" and joint groups had worked on developing creative integrative games for Jewish and Palestinian children. The enterprise was funded by Mousa Halil's foundation in Malmo, Sweden, and Moshe Galil, from the vicinity of Tel Aviv, Israel, was in charge of its creative management.

As a result of the wonderful public relations activities promoting the

"ISLAEL" enterprise, run jointly in Europe by Leila Halil and Ronit Galil, the creative and integrative games were already being implemented in five European countries, attended by children of both nations.

The original exciting games had managed to create multi-cultural social and ethical relationships among Jews and Arabs as well as between other ethnic groups in conflict areas all over the world.

The Swedish award committee held the ceremony, for a change, not at the prestigious convention palace in the Swedish capital but rather facing… the sculpture of the mermaid in Copenhagen, as a gesture to the unusual winners.

Mousa Halil and Moshe Galil founded an incredibly successful global social organization named "Hagalil". At this time they are still going strong, receiving many appeals from all over the world to create integrative children's games.

Leila and Ronit devote a significant part of their time to volunteering to promote these projects in conflict and war-ridden regions all over the world. They have recently received a proposal to run a giant welfare project in Africa, financed by Scandinavian funds, and have happily consented.

The only thing in our world that is impossible is 'the impossible'. This is also true of human relationships.

16

A Short Transatlantic Story

● ● ●

That morning Rick Scott, an American, returned to his home in Long Island, New York, from another of his trips to Siena, Italy. By the evening he was already at a party with Jenny, his tall dazzling American girlfriend. She picked him up from his house, a short drive from her own.

At the party he met Chuck, a former classmate from the drama department of a prestigious art college. They had not seen each other in about four years. It was a good time to fill each other in on their life during the long period of separation. The two spoke for several minutes. Chuck told his friend that he was still a frustrated playwright whose plays had not been accepted by any serious theater, and wanted to explain further… but suddenly Rick interrupted him. He decided to take advantage of the fact that both their dates were at an improvised beauty workshop with a popular beauty consultant at the other side of the spacious garden. He preferred to talk to his friend about the last day than about the last years… The truth was that he urgently needed to tell someone he knew about events during the past day, which seemed to him very strange. He didn't want the women to show up in the middle of his story. So he interrupted his friend.

Chuck was the right person to share his experiences with, a pleasant interlocutor, with a good sense of humor. He also had nice memories from the days when he and Rick had hung out with a regular group of students at the vibrant and fashionable clubs of the Village in Manhattan.

"I'll tell you a story. I returned today from Siena, Italy, where I spent a week with my Italian girlfriend Tonia at her home... Yes, Chuck, I see that you remember from school that I believe in living life to the full. My approach to life has not changed, so I arranged for myself two girlfriends, one on each side of the Atlantic. Neither of them knew about the other. Even more interesting and not by chance, Tonia looks almost exactly like Jenny. The same body structure, the same hair, the same gaze, the same eyes, even the same smile. That's how I chose them. Jenny is an American of Italian descent. Tonia is an Italian of American descent..." Unsurprisingly, Chuck was fascinated by his former friend's description of his current life style with a girl on each side of the ocean. But then he became even more enthralled by Rick's story. Even when they had studied together and after completing their studies, he had been amazed at Rick's success with women. His admiration had been combined at times with a certain natural jealousy. Chuck, unlike Rick, was a one-woman guy, whose relationships lasted for several years.

"Tonia drove me to the airport in Rome, and on the way we stopped at a magnificent field of irises. We made love on the colorful carpet with unlimited passion, a latonic experience that stayed with me until I boarded the plane..."

"Latonic. I like that. A winning combination of Tonia and Latino, right?!

"Exactly. I love combinations and that's why I'm combining my drama studies with psychology. As I told you before I greatly enjoy my career in psychotherapy. That's how I met Tonia at the university at Siena, where I was a visiting facilitator. I had just ended another concurrent relationship with someone else in New York... and I replaced her with Tonia, Jenny's double... When I landed at Kennedy Airport I was met by Jenny. I asked her to meet me in the parking lot. On the way to our home in Long Island we had passionate sex in the car. We both could not wait to get home... In those moments I couldn't decide what was more exciting and who had excited me more, the student at the airport in Italy or the lecturer in the car in America..." Rick spoke quickly. He wanted to end his story before their dates returned.

"Wow, what a story!" Chuck admired his former friend's juicy description. He had never heard anything like it.

In a little while he regained his composure and then he said with typical satirical humor: "Rick, but you still had a problem. The ten hour trip from Italy to New York must have been quite a trial..."

"Not at all!" Rick answered, as if he had anticipated Chuck's question.

"That is where the real story begins…"

"What…", Chuck could not hide his amazement, "there's more?!"

"Three female friends, Italian graduate students of the arts, were on the flight. They were on their way to a long weekend in New York. Two of them sat several rows in front of me. And the third, the most beautiful, sat in my three-seat row where I occupied the window seat. She had the aisle seat, and the middle seat was empty… And guess what happened between me and that Italian student… and it's not what you think…"

"Right, there's only one thing I could think of, I could imagine…"

"So listen to the amazing thing that happened to me after we took off, once the seatbelt light was off… The beautiful Italian and myself folded back our armrests and sat closer to each other. I drew her to me…"

"That's just what I was thinking. Why did you say that I couldn't imagine what happened?" Chuck interrupted him.

"Wait a second, it's still not what you think… Under cover of the blanket she said to me, in a most direct manner: 'I will not flirt with you. I know that you have an American girlfriend. I read all the text messages she sent you while we were making love. You were so sure that I wouldn't find out. You weren't even careful. I have no wish to get involved with a man who has another relationship. I want to be a one-man woman, even if he's American… Making love in the field was my farewell gift. I will spend four beautiful days with my friends in New York, and please don't contact me again, neither there nor anywhere else. By the way, you could have told your girlfriend to come to the welcoming area and not to the parking lot. I know that you were concerned that she would see us together. Don't worry, it won't happen. Now please take the blanket off us…"

"One minute, stop. How did your Italian girl know that you have an American girlfriend…?"

"A little patience and you'll hear it all. The impressive young woman added to her direct statement: 'I accessed your cellular phone and saw everything. That was after you disappeared at the Armando restaurant at the square in Siena, and then I had my suspicions…"

"Wow, Rick, a winning story for a book of short stories, or for a play, and it has almost everything: erotica, drama, trans-Atlantic cheating, beautiful women, adventures, the crazy fantasy of finding two identical lovers, and also the fall of a macho. In addition, it has a surprising development involving one of the main characters in the 'surreal play'. You must have paid close attention in our classes with Professor Edna Parton, head of the drama department…"

Chuck suddenly felt that he had the basis to realize his personal dream, to write a play, with all the elements that he had just identified in Rick's story.

"You've given me a great idea for a play... I'll think of the most dramatic ending possible..."

And that moment, when Chuck was at the height of his enthusiasm, thinking of how he would realize his dream, their dates, who had completed the improvised beauty workshop, returned full of interesting experiences, and not only from the workshop.

"Can I interrupt you for a moment?" Jenny asked Rick: "You must have had an interesting nostalgic conversation. Now I too have an interesting topic to discuss with you, my dear. Chuck, can I 'steal' Rick from you for a few minutes? I'll bring him back right away, and then he'll be yours for as long as you like..."

Jenny held onto his right arm gently, "Come close, I want to whisper something important, even very important..."

Chuck and his date Kim followed the other couple and sensed in their body movements that something was happening.

"I know everything. While we were at the beauty workshop I had a telephone call from your former student, Tonia. You must know her well..."

"Did she also tell you what happened to our relationship on the plane last night?"

"Yes. For me it's too late, too little, and too uninteresting, and it's over. Thanks. You can go back to Chuck. I'm going home alone. Come pick up your things tomorrow. Call me tomorrow and I'll tell you when I'll be out... Thanks for two nice years. I'll only remember the good moments. Don't try to talk me out of it. I forgave you the last time you cheated on me. This was once too many."

Jenny said a short goodbye to the other couple and left the man she had rejected, as though she had never been there. In the cab she felt liberated, and managed to overcome her strong emotions.

Rick went over to Chuck, gave him his card, and said: "Call me tomorrow, I have an incredible end for your play..."

Kim also said goodbye to Rick, and then said to Chuck her boyfriend: "In the middle of the beauty workshop Jenny received a telephone call. She left us for seven or ten minutes. We were surprised at her absence and that it took her a while to return. She was very upset. I left the workshop with her to support her. You don't have to call Rick tomorrow. I'll tell you all about it tonight. She told me about her shocking telephone conversation with Rick's Italian lover … Don't worry, my love, you'll have a fascinating dramatic end to your play…"

Nine months after he met Rick at the party, Chuck Acton realized the dream of his life. He won acclaim as a successful playwright. His play, 'Between an Italian lover and an American girlfriend,' was staged with great success at a well-known Off Broadway theater. He changed the names of the characters in Rick's story but retained all the inspiration Rick had given him…

Better one bird on one side of the ocean than one on each side...

17

"I've waited 40 years for this moment..."

• • •

"Mr. Cary Kukuchi, aim the video camera right at me!... I've waited 40 years for this moment. Four decades I've wished for an opportunity to say something important about you and me during our high school years; since the tenth grade."

Ichiro Mipona's voice was just as authoritative as it had been in their popular high school in the prestigious quarter of Osaka, Japan. Mipona was one of the class leaders and everyone had expected him to do well in life, maybe more than all his classmates. So no one was surprised when this impressive man, who towered above his classmates, appeared at their 40th anniversary with the title of a regional European director of a giant global media corporation, a high international rank.

The private corporation was owned by businessmen and wealthy people from the Far East, with an annual profit margin estimated at several billion dollars.

Only people with excellent management abilities and great personal charisma reached the position of senior director at this giant corporation. Dr. Ichiro Mipona was one of the most prominent. The man had realized all expectations, even when his surname was still Murami and his friends called him Chiroki.

Cary Kukuchi was the complete opposite of Ichiro Mipona. Their classmates paid him no attention and he had been the 'punching bag' of the class leaders, and particularly of Ichiro who abused him emotionally. It was often maltreatment for its own sake, and it made things very unpleasant for Cary.

After three years of ridicule and mental abuse Ichiro the bully fell into a hole dug in the earth near the entrance to his home. He fell in the dark, and for six months his leg remained in a cast. His leg was broken, as was his status in the class.

Ichiro and some of his friends suspected Kukuchi of sending his two brothers to plan this trick as an act of revenge. The latter denied that he had anything to do with it, whether directly or indirectly. He also claimed that he did not even know Ichiro's address. Indeed, it was never proven that Cary had been involved in any way in his abuser's fall and injury.

Some of the graduates who had gathered for the nostalgic reunion at the high-class hotel in Osaka were surprised to see Cary Kukuchi among them. Energetic Tasuki, who had organized the gathering, had insisted on inviting all her classmates. She left no one out. She even reached the Virgin Islands (by e-mail), where one of the graduates was living, using the social and business networks in order to plan the successful evening, assisted by Rika, her childhood friend. Tasuki somehow managed to inform Cary Kukuchi of the event, through a third party. Cary himself was amazed that the organizer had managed to reach him through an intermediate. He came to the event from afar. Only he knew how important it was for him to be here and what a surprise he had brought with him.

His classmates assumed that he still held a grudge against some of his peers for pushing him aside and bullying him, a matter of general knowledge that sometimes even required the intervention of the head of the school. The graduates did not perceive him as part of the class, one that had produced successful professionals such as senior doctors, successful project managers, renowned artists, and even inventors who left their mark on Japanese hi-tech and in Silicon Valley in California. Yes, it was a special class. Both its male and female graduates had attained success.

The innovative Sony video camera operated by Cary Kukuchi seemed to some of those in doubt a good solution, enabling him to attend the reunion while in a subservient position, videotaping the event without really being part of it. It was seen as a way of remaining on the margins, as he had always done. This, at least, was the opinion of some who were surprised by his appearance at the posh restaurant on the roof of the famous towers. Even now he was perceived as 'an outsider' by those who still couldn't accept him. They saw him as the equivalent of a wedding photographer who had come to work rather than being invited as a guest. Tasuki the organizer was very nice to Cary Kukuchi throughout the evening. Yumi, formerly the belle of the class and the only one who despite many suitors was still single, was very excited to see him. In general, the girls in the class were more accepting than most of the male graduates. The truth was that no one knew what Cary Kukuchi did for a living. But in the excited mingling with friends at the bar, some of whom had not seen each other for decades(!), a rumor began circulating that he mostly lived abroad and was involved in mysterious and unknown business. They expected things to clear up during the evening, when each of them in turn would speak of his or her life and history throughout the last four decades.

Indeed, after the good meal, with the plentiful sake, each in turn was asked by the moderator, affable comic Harada, to tell everyone a little about his or her life since graduation and also something that they remembered from their school days, when Osaka was a budding financial city.
The teacher, Mrs. Sakura Yoki, who looked very lively, as though time had stopped for her, was given the honor of being the first to speak. Excited, she said that she was happy to have been invited. She said that from her experience it is hard to anticipate who will be more or less successful in life based on personal academic achievements and failures. In this context, she estimated that when those present spoke of their status in life everyone would be surprised, whether pleasantly or not so much. She remained direct and honest in her approach and sharp-tongued, as she had been throughout her four years with them in high school. Theirs was the first class in which she had served as homeroom teacher. The applause that followed her words was very generous, for good reason. She devoted an entire part of her words to Japan's achievements over the last forty years, and how Japan's Zen Buddhism had contributed to the flourishing of the local economy and attracted supporters all over the world. She said that just as they had learned the principles of Japanese Zen at school, during their adult life they had surely realized – so she said – how the Buddhist approach of provocative challenges with a Zen outlook had enhanced the creativity of its graduates. That was her assumption.

Ten or maybe a dozen graduates spoke in turn, proceeding clockwise. Some stories were fascinating and others were a little vague and even disappointing, describing mediocre life achievements.

Then it was the turn of Dr. Ichiro Mipona, the class star, at least judging by his achievements, which received constant coverage in the financial press and sometimes even as a general news item in the Japanese or global media.
"Forty years", he began, speaking passionately, "I have been waiting for this moment"…
His words aroused everyone's curiosity, eager to know what the senior director wished to reveal to the man photographing him now at the event, forty years after their graduation. Why did he ask Cary so dramatically to aim the camera at him and record his words with the video camera on its tripod?
Two people, two extremities, and so many years in the middle, including several wars. Does he intend to say that he will never forgive Cary for setting him a trap, that he still believes that Cary was involved? Maybe it is something else: Does the tall successful man want to take his revenge on Cary Kukuchi, who several years after graduating dared to 'hit on' Ichiro's sister at a discotheque and court her, to his chagrin? The mere thought had been worthy of reproach, according to the star of the class. And maybe Ichiro wanted to remind Cary of the beating he had received from Cary's big brother when they returned from their final school trip, a beating that might have left him with a mental scar to this very day? Who knows, maybe he would make one of these statements with a conciliatory tone.
Some wondered whether the curse and the threat leveled at Kukuchi in the twelfth grade, in the presence of everyone, when 'Chachiroki', as he was called by his friends, first acquired confidence and put an end to the abuse, were what the successful CEO remembered. Did that constitutive event still weigh on him, four decades later?! In terms of his impressive success he must have forgotten it long ago, not so?! It was hard to estimate the meaning of the drama created by the successful man, and what significance could still possibly be attached to any reckoning forty years after graduation.

Many of the graduates still remembered the words of their teacher, Mrs. Sakura Yoki, at the beginning of the tenth grade: 'The industrious will succeed, the lazy will lag behind', a Buddhist idea that the esteemed teacher was fond of stressing.

The curiosity and tension among the classmates reached a high: Where would the demand lead, Ichiro's command to Cary to level the camera at him and record him with the state-of-the-art camera?!

Would the historical clock freeze and would the humiliation and bullying of the dominant leader versus the guerrilla acts of the 'peripheral student' recur, taking them all back to their high school years? They were reminded of the conflict initiated by the 'golden boy' of the past, who had it all, against the son of the inferior family, who was forced to make his way in the class and fight like an alley cat to survive, at times surprising everyone with the deviousness of his reactions.

In another incident in those days Cary, against all odds, had managed to attract Misa, the 'sexiest' girl in class… courted by most of the boys. This surprising attraction between the 'belle' of the class and the second-rate student was reminiscent of the West Side Story, or of other similar stories.

Misa, who had once sported dimples, jumped out of her chair with all her current day wrinkles, and with a passion that had never left her said: "Just keep me out of it. I've been divorced once, widowed once, and I came to this reunion all the way from Beverly Hills… so no verbal or other violence, please. In any case, I too have a secret from the 11th grade that only one person in this class is aware of… I'll reveal it at our 50th anniversary reunion. Not today." The atmosphere was extremely tense, it could have been cut with the penknife produced by Fat Eli, who had brought it to show everyone, as a nostalgic item. It was a dark red penknife that had remained with him all these years and reminded him that at least in one thing he was the best in class – and that was throwing a penknife at circles drawn in the sand.

Silver haired Dr. Ichiro Mipona recovered from Misa's spontaneous outburst. He placed both hands on his chest and, staring at the video camera on the tripod, said in a low voice that he had decided that this was the proper moment to repay the debt he owed Cary from many years ago. All his attending classmates deserved to hear this revelation… it was the right time and place.

In the first sentence, addressed to Cary Kukuchi, he produced his 'bombshell' and said outright: "I owe you, Mr. Kukuchi, a big a-p-o-l-o-g-y and I also owe you many of my life's insights that brought me to where I am today…"

All those present were amazed by this shocking and unexpected overture, as was the teacher, who was enthralled by each of Ichiro's words. The successful European director continued: "I thought a lot about our mental abuse of you when my young son Taki told me, in tears, that he is not popular in class, and that his classmates reject him. Then I understood how badly I had behaved towards you. This insight helped me understand how I should treat people regardless of their background and abilities, with more respect. I suddenly understood that a blow to the soul can be extremely cruel. I understood that life can take its revenge on you for your bad deeds… I learned the power of an honest apology and of a real request for forgiveness. I felt very bad for what I had done to you. Throughout my professional career I thought of my guilt, of my responsibility for your feelings of rejection and humiliation. I also understood that words have cruel power. I learned that being considerate is more important than making others consider your importance…"

All the graduates seated around the table were astounded…

"You can't imagine, dear Mr. Kukuchi, how eagerly I anticipated this wonderful moment, the opportunity to apologize to you from the bottom of my heart… forty apologies – one for every year. Sorry, Cary. Sorry, sorry, sorry."

Quite a few of the adults at the reunion were crying by now. Their teacher, Mrs. Sakura Yoki, had the most trouble holding back her tears. The applause that followed the senior director's confession went on for several minutes. And everything was recorded, of course, by the first-class Japanese video camera wielded by Cary Kukuchi, 'the second-rate kid', who had only become more handsome with each passing year. The decades had modified his garbled accent and unclear speech, which now had a foreign lilt, slightly American, but not fully defined.

Rika, remembered as one of the quieter girls in class, could not restrain herself. Right after the applause for Ichiko's amazing words, she got up, put her hands on Cary's shoulders, kissed him softly on the cheek, and said: "Cary Kukuchi, my dearest friend, now it's your turn." She asked Dr. Mipona to take charge of the camera on its tripod while Cary would take his seat and tell his story.

"To tell you the truth, Dr. Mipona, I too owe you something that I have been carrying with me for a long time, for many years since life began to look up for me. And this debt is… a big t-h-a-n-k y-o-u. To follow your lead, forty thank yous, one for each year since we graduated… the challenges you created for me strengthened and forged me, my character, and my personality. What you did to me forced me to choose: to give up or to go on. Thanks to you I made the right choice in life. Yes, it was a choice. I chose to fight and succeed, rather than to flee and fail…"

Even the waiters and the barmen held their breath at the unfolding drama. All the attending graduates were amazed and astounded by the revelations and by their impressive presentation by the 'second-rate kid' they had known four decades ago, the student who had barely managed to complete his studies.

The wise teacher was once again right. This was definitely not what they had expected of Kukuchi, the rejected boy. The successful proud doctor was moved and excited, recording Cary Kukuchi's monologue that had taken everyone by surprise…

The drama in the high-class restaurant, at the class reunion, continued to break all records, bringing with it the next unbelievable revelation, the most amazing possible in these circumstances.

"My character was forged thanks to you, my dear friend, leading to a job as security guard for businessmen, unidentified tycoons, once I had completed my army service. As a result, quite a few years ago I saved the life of a Singapore billionaire who insisted on Japanese bodyguards. In circumstances that must remain hidden, I saved his life. He promoted me in his business. In time I quietly advanced in the business world of our developing continent. I went to university in Singapore. I travelled widely throughout our continent, and gradually became one of the owners of a global Singaporean-Malaysian corporation…"

Everybody in the restaurant held their collective breath. Each word uttered by Mr. Cary Kukuchi held everyone mesmerized.

"For years I haven't had a visible role in the corporation's management. The manager of the unit in charge of 'hunting down' senior directors for the organization provides me with the CVs of all candidates for senior management positions, their recommendations, results of their evaluations, and I decide, behind the scenes, who will be appointed to the dozen management roles: six regional directors and six directors in the corporation's headquarters. I made sure that my name was not publicly mentioned as one of the corporation's owners, neither on the internet or anywhere else…

When we were searching for a regional director in Europe four years ago, the recruitment director for senior positions brought me the files of the five candidates who had reached the final stage. Only one of them was Japanese, I. When I saw his name and read his CV, including his age, although his surname had changed I knew that I had been given a chance from heaven, anticipated for many years, to thank him and appoint… my dear friend Dr. Ichiro Mipona as the regional director in Europe of our corporation, Eastern Western Great Communication…
That was my way of thanking you, my beloved friend, for helping me reach my current position. And you knew nothing about it".

The term 'multiple shock' was suddenly insufficient to describe the sensation of the graduates when Cary Kukuchi finished speaking.

The mythical teacher with her noble appearance thought that she had experienced everything in her forty years as a teacher, with hundreds of students and their parents, working with dozens of teachers and supervisors. That's what she had thought, but this evening she realized that she was wrong, this unforgettable evening. And in light of the incredible drama, she was overjoyed that she had begun her career as a homeroom teacher with this special 9th grade. This evening she had received a 'bonus' in the form of an unparalleled life experience.

Before everyone got up to leave, Cary Kukuchi, the unwavering star of the evening, thanked Tasuki Mizuki, manager of a big network of department stores in Fukuoka, Southern Japan. She had organized this charming and amazing reunion and had spared no effort to reach him. He further asked her if she would like a vacation with her husband on the island of Bali in Indonesia…
Tasuki, the elegant lady, was very happy and accepted the business card he gave her to coordinate the trip of her dreams.

All the other participants in the remarkable event requested and received

Cary Kukuchi's silver business card as a memento of the outstanding reunion. The card stated his name in English, with a mobile phone number and an e-mail address. No company or corporation was mentioned. No job description or title, and not even the country from which the card's owner originated…

Two words that do so much for us in life are 'sorry' and 'thanks'. Even more so: 'so sorry' and 'thank you very much'.

18

The lonely Georgian and the magnificent carpet from the Caucasus

● ● ●

Tom Thomas had done all he could, tried out every possible method, trick, and twist to win Yana's heart. The young woman who had charmed him was a beautiful talented 24 year old pianist.

This was the first time in all his 31 years that Tom had been in love. For a month and a half he had made every effort to court her. Yana had not rejected his attempts completely, but then she had also not really responded to them. She evaded him with various excuses that sometimes even sounded logical and justified: Her mother was ill and needed her attention; a concert she was giving at the Northridge community center required lots of rehearsals and took a great deal of her time, and also a music project in which she was participating in a disadvantaged area was reaching its conclusion and her involvement was cheering up children from poor families.

Tom had never given up on his aims at any stage in life, at school, in the army, at university, in his professional career, or in his social activities. The latter included his volunteer work at an association for destitute elderly people, where he had happened to meet Yana at a charity event.

She herself had volunteered to give a piano recital for the seniors, mostly singles who enjoyed the input of generous people such as Yana and Tom. He had volunteered to give his fascinating lectures and stories for their benefit.

In the few telephone conversations he managed to hold with her and in their e-mail correspondence, he discovered that Yana's Georgian roots occupied her and were a source of pride and preservation of the family tradition. Her parents had immigrated from Georgia to Los Angeles before she was born. They had joined relatives who had been living in a tiny Georgian community in the San Fernando Valley in LA for several generations. She even told him, in an e-mail written a week ago, that she had the honor of being a descendant of Mousa al-Taflisi, founder of the Taflisi Karaite cult, said to originate from Georgia. He saw this revelation not only as a piece of information but maybe as the beginning of some sort of response on her part.

Tom was always optimistic. When lecturing for his company, he would ask his audience rhetorically about the difference between pessimists and optimists. And then he would answer: "A pessimist constantly suffers. An optimist, however, enjoys many pleasures until encountering a single disappointment." This was his worldview, and more than that, his approach to life.

Since beginning his courtship of Yana Tom Thomas had sent her a magnificent bouquet every Friday, and he had also sent her by messenger an impressive English album on the Georgian community in the United States and its heritage. He bought the book at a special shop specializing in folklore and world culture. The album was delivered with a bottle of Georgian wine bought at a Georgian delicatessen in downtown Los Angeles. Tom also posted on his website: 'To all those interested: I'm no longer available. I've finally found the love of my life and her name is Yana. I hope that she will love me too.'

Even when interviewed on the financial section of a radio program about his specialty, investment in foreign stock exchanges, he mentioned Yana anonymously. He said that he himself is investing in an option… a very pretty and talented artist, and this investment is aimed at forming a relationship and a family. Tom ordered a transcript of the long interview, scanned it, and e-mailed it to the young woman who had captured his heart. He highlighted his remark about her. She answered that she was impressed by the gesture but 'at the moment', she said, 'I'm not ready for a relationship'.

Some words 'leave room for hope'. 'At the moment' and 'not at the moment' are good examples. 'At the moment I'm not ready...' left room for Tom's next creative idea.

And so, four days and several telephone calls and e-mails later, Tom decided to take action. Maybe, he hoped, his plan would manage to overcome Yana's barriers. He bought a plane ticket to Tbilisi, the capital of Georgia.

After many hours on the plane he landed in 'Paris of Asia', as defined by the private driver-guide he hired in the Georgian capital, recommended by a friend. He settled in at a pleasant modern hotel and from there planned his conquest of Tbilisi and nearby parts of Georgia, together with the affable guide. More than that, he planned his conquest of Yana's heart in a military operation that traversed Georgia. That was always his way. He was adamant, decisive, effortful, goal-oriented, and would do anything to reach his aims. This time, winning Yana's heart was his most important personal goal, although it would be hard to achieve. Very hard, but not impossible. At least so he thought.

* * *

29 year old Mikhail Tobishvili, a successful carpet manufacturer and merchant from Tbilisi, knew that he had betrayed the trust of those closest to him. They wanted him to marry a family relative who had been introduced to him. The episode had taken place after his graduation from the foreign trade college in Tbilisi. He knew that his punishment for refusing was seclusion and separation from his extensive family. He reached an agreement with his parents that he would continue working in the family's carpet business, with its reputation formed over seven generations.

He suffered a torturous loneliness. From time to time he would find solace at the ancient Greek Orthodox church near his business. This was where he found temporary refuge from his loneliness. The location of his business, beside the church with its impressive façade and wealth of inner treasures, attracted to his business many tourists from all over the world. Tom Thomas came there as well with his guide, who was well acquainted with Mikhail and received a commission for any purchases made by tourists he brought.

The learned carpet merchant, with his humane warmth, loved to listen to stories. His loneliness in recent years only increased this yearning.

Through the stories he would sail for distant places, and this was a replacement, a type of solution to his inability to take a vacation from his business. Since the family lesson he had learned he made certain to conduct himself fairly with anyone with whom he came in contact.

Mikhail designed his carpets tastefully and employed weavers, spinners, and embroiderers for his carpets in nearby Caucasian villages. He paid them a salary that enabled them to live comfortably. He sold the products with their magnificent design and high quality finish to tourists at a reasonable profit. Tour guides were aware of his love of stories, and from time to time they came to have coffee with him when things were quiet, telling him stories they had heard from their tourists. Sometimes he himself managed to hear a story from articulate tourists who visited his business. He had a display hall with an incredible array of carpets that left many visitors open mouthed. Some tourists made purchases, usually buying the smaller carpets, but most only admired the display and the demonstration of the carpets' weaving and finish. The visit left them with an impression of art and skill, passed down through generations of the Tobishvili family and of the Caucasian families he employed.

Tom, who arrived at Mikhail's business with his guide, was immediately captivated, upon entering, by an outstanding carpet with a combination of turquoise, scarlet, and gold, and a central motif of two hearts. A Caucasian carpet that was a real work of art. The price asked was astronomical in Georgian terms. Mikhail was asking $900 for the work of art that had attracted Tom's attention. The American tourist knew that this carpet would have great significance for his life. This knowledge was part of the plan he had spun. Some spin carpets, Tom spun plans. The carpet was part of the plot he was spinning.

In his conversations with Yana before his trip, she had told him about her 'fetish', her craze for artistic Asian carpets. "Bingo", he said to himself, looking at the carpet and stroking it. "This is the 'magic carpet' with the two hearts that will take me to her…"

While he was still thinking about it and considering the sum necessary to purchase the expensive carpet, the mobile telephone held by Mikhail, the young lonely Georgian, began to ring. Tom was amazed at the ringtone. He couldn't believe it. It was his father's favorite song. Tom always loved to hear this song. Several years ago he had watched a 'movie of his parents' generation', which young people of his age still appreciated. It included erotic scenes with a fragrance of youthful romance. This movie, still popular in Germany, Japan, and other countries, 'Eskimo Lemon I', ended with the song featured in the ringtone. The song, 'Mr. Lonely', Bobby Winton's legendary song, always excited viewers and listeners.

Mikhail quickly ended his short telephone conversation. He jumped at the opportunity offered by Tom to tell him the story of the movie concluding with the song in the ringtone. Tom was an extremely captivating storyteller. He was touched by the story of the loneliness of one of the movie's main characters, who remained solitary at the end of the plot. Loneliness was 'the story of his life', after his family clan left him, rejected him.

Of all the stories he had ever heard from tourists or guides this was the best, the closest to his heart. He identified so closely with the lonely character in the film that his eyes began to tear. It seemed to him that for the three years since he had severed all ties with his family and been punished by loneliness and estrangement he had not been so moved.

Tom asked Mikhail to embroider within the central drawing the words 'To Yana the pianist with love' and this took only two hours. He compensated the embroiderer generously for her work.

The incredibly unique and beautiful carpet was packed carefully and flown to Los Angeles that same day. Its price was the icing on the cake. Mikhail gave Tom the carpet in return for his moving story for the cost of production, only $300. That was what he had paid the Caucasian family who toiled over the carpet for two weeks. His profit was his excitement at hearing the story, the equivalent of the $600 that he had deducted from the initial price quoted before the phone rang…

Tom landed in Los Angeles after a long and tiring flight full of impressions of the country that seemed to him the ultimate Garden of Eden. The morning after his arrival a representative of the global delivery company came to deliver the carpet. That evening Tom and the carpet were at Yana's apartment. She was very moved by the generous gesture. But to his disappointment and even dismay she refused to receive the carpet that declared Tom's love for her. She told him very honestly that although she does like and admire him she does not love him.

Yana was impressed by the carpet and the dedication embroidered on it, but even more by Mikhail Tobishvili who, touched by Tom's special story, had given him the expensive carpet. She felt intuitively that Mikhail must be a rare human being… and he may certainly be the man she was seeking. And he was even from her own culture and ethnic group.

Using the information Tom had given her about the carpet seller she managed to find Mikhail at her own initiative on her social network. She asked him to be her friend.

The relationship between the two developed rapidly. The messengers of the international transport company were kept busy, and Yana's house filled with exciting items associated with her Georgian heritage. She herself sent him a CD of Georgian melodies that she had composed. She also dedicated a song to him, written and put to music in his honor: 'Mikhail, my man in Tbilisi.'

The relationship between Mikhail and Yana was intensive, rapid, and productive. He invited her to his beautiful home in Tbilisi. She took the chance and did not hesitate to make the trip. The virtual relationship matured into a real romance.

Yana, with her special talents, managed to mend the schism between Mikhail and his family. They made their peace with their son and... fell in love with her.

Ten months after the evening when Yana first heard Mikhail's story from Tom and rejected his gift of the carpet, she married her beloved from Tbilisi. It was a magnificent joyous Georgian wedding, held at a charming events' complex, the 'Marriage Carpet', in downtown Los Angeles.

The reconciled members of Mikhail's 'clan' came to the happy lavish wedding. They filled half a plane from Tbilisi to LAX.

Yana's mother recovered, mainly thanks to her joy at her amazing daughter.

Tom and his beloved fiancé Bella were guests of honor at the wedding. The gift they brought was an original one and they didn't even have to buy it. The wedding gift had been saved from that amazing evening. A professional embroiderer had embroidered a new message in the hearts at the center of the carpet. The new words were:

'To our dear Yana and Mikhail
With our deepest thanks and love
Bella and Tom'

That evening, when Tom had come to Yana's home after his trip, another dramatic incident had followed her rejection of Tom and his gift of the carpet… she suggested that he call her twin sister, who was almost identical to her. She had a good feeling that once again her intuition would not be wrong. Bella, her twin sister, had consented in advance to Yana's offer to introduce her to Tom.

The next morning Tom called Bella, Yana's nearly identical twin sister. That same evening they met.

Bella fell in love with Tom at first sight. It was the first time that she had felt such a wonderful sense of infatuation.

Bella was the second love of Tom's life. And the first to fall for him with her entire soul.

The two consummated their love at a wedding held the following week, where the roles were reversed. This time Yana and Mikhail Tobishvili were the guests of honor. This wedding was held at the popular 'Wedding Wonders' hall on the beach of Santa Monica, the city of angels.

'When someone says he is feeling lonely, he's not lying'. You can take his word for it.

19

The real drama
is in the lecture hall
(and not in the film)

• • •

At the end of the lecture, entitled 'What gives a film its drama?,' Lily took a good look at the local lecture hall. Most of those who had attended the series, which combined lectures with films, were women aged 45-65, and some were men accompanying their wives, often as an act of goodwill. Although the lecture given by the doctor of cinema had fascinated the 300 people in the audience, the woman with her beautifully apportioned body, outstanding for her age, did not seem to feel part of it all. Her young appearance managed to cut several years off, but her face could not hide the tempest that raged within her at the sight of the lecturer on stage. She had unexpectedly noticed, one row below her, in her peripheral vision, a man she had been involved with in the past. This vague relationship had led to heartfelt soulful deliberations, followed by the sense of a missed opportunity, one that had remained with her for many years, almost until the current evening.

Throughout the entire series given at this lecture hall, a series called 'The real story' that was now nearing its end, Lily had been fascinated by the lectures. But this evening was an exception.

For the first time Lily, usually a calm and stable person, felt as if she was somewhere else completely, occupied with her own personal drama rather than the lecture. An emotional sense of 'here and now' pervaded the hall. Only she recognized it for what it was. She felt that she was suddenly being drawn back many years to her youth, a period so distant from today's anti-ageing treatments that were completely unknown at the time, certainly not part of the personal consciousness of our protagonist Lily, who had once justly earned the nickname 'Maxi sexy'. She had always known how to show off her legs, wearing a maxi miniskirt.

Her former friends had always taken it for granted that with her luscious feminine looks as a teenager she would become a famous performer on the stage or in the cinema. Her friends and sisters were even more certain when one outstanding evening she dared to evade the security people, jumping up on stage at a concert given by a British rock star who had come to perform at the mythological Vista cinema. She had her moment of glory when she managed to hug the legendary youth idol who even kissed her on the cheek. The incident lasted several seconds, astounding the audience and completely surprising the skilled security team stationed around the stage. It even earned a news item in the press and in the cinema news journal. At her high school in Santa Barbara it was the most publicized incident that year. But this was the culmination of Lily's performances on stage.

As a young lady many young men, and some not so young, were attracted to her. It began at the end of the tenth grade. As the young and older men increased their attempts to court her, so did her longing to prove to everyone that her inner beauty was even stronger than the external. When she was 16 she read the book 'Beautiful character', which in a section on the importance of inner beauty says:

'External beauty
is minimized
when encountering
inner
beauty
measured
mainly
by your own
self-measure!'

She liked this thought and it appeared to have quite an effect on the course of her life. She photocopied the section and had it enlarged and framed. It occupied a place of honor in her room, and in time in her home office, and then at the prestigious academic institute where she became a renowned scholar.

As the lecture in the hall that evening progressed towards its conclusion, to be followed by a break and then the screening of a drama, her inner turmoil grew.

Finally it was time for the break. A large part of the audience rushed to the snack bar and the restrooms. Lily remained in her seat. Her two girlfriends felt that something was wrong. They too remained in their seats and asked Lily if she was okay. The two, who had known her for many years, realized that their friend had not been 'focused' on the lecture that constituted the first part of the event. The two attempted to try and find out what had happened to their 'wandering' friend. But suddenly their attempt to prompt her came to a halt even before it had begun. Hilary, who was in charge of the lecture series, appeared. She had known Lily for a long time and addressed her first, only then turning to the other two. Hilary was incredibly professional and a perfectionist. She always took advantage of the 30 minute break to gather feedback on each lecturer from the audience. In these conversations, she inquired whether they were satisfied with the content of the lecture, its mode of conveyance, and the techniques used by the lecturer. She even asked for their opinion on the lecturer's personal appearance.

"How was the lecture on drama?" Hilary asked. Lily remained distracted, as though she had not heard the question. Marilyn was the first to reply. She said that she had enjoyed it very much, and was glad to say that it had been informative. She was particularly impressed, she said, when the film expert demonstrated how a comedy can also be a drama. The lecturer had said that this is how the film genre of dramatic comedy had evolved. She had one critical comment on the lecturer's attire, to be exact his baggy checked pants which, in her opinion, were inappropriate. Lily's other friend, Mabel, had enjoyed herself as well, but as an English linguist she criticized the lecturer for his use of Latin terms. They all waited for Lily to speak, as she was the most successful professional careerist of the three. Finally she smiled slightly, lifted her gaze, and answered Hilary's original question with a query of her own: "Was it a lecture on drama?!" She paused slightly. All three women expected her to go on, and then she muttered, half to herself and half out loud: "For me the drama is neither in the lecture nor in the film to follow... for me the real drama is in the lecture hall… and it, I mean he, is sitting right there in the row in front of us, five or six seats to the left." Lily managed to create a surreal drama of her own within the encounter on films and drama, at least for the four of them.

The seeds of this drama, now raging in Lily's heart, had been sown many years ago in the form of a romantic relationship of two couples, which began at an intersection leading down to the marina in beautiful Santa Barbara. This place was a convergence of two streets commemorating two impressive personages. One was named for a well known Spanish author and poet, and the other for a famous French scientist. In this respect Santa Barbara was indeed a city that brought together Spanish culture, a French way of life, and a contemporary American atmosphere. An impressive Chrysler had appeared at the time, many years ago, from the east, from the direction of the beach. Nineteen year old Tommy with his sharp eyes identified the 'feminine potential,' noticing two impressive young ladies armed with fashionable sunglasses about 20 meters from his car. He stopped the shiny American car he had taken from his parents for a 'short ride', coming to a standstill with two wheels on the pavement. The squeal of his brakes still reverberated as he turned to his good friend Freddy beside him, and with a victorious look said: "I knew we'd come up with two girls for the party at Nicky's. I knew, but I didn't believe we'd find such 'hot chicks'. You see? It's a good thing I insisted that you switch your weekend duties and do your guard duty last week instead of today, so that we could be together for the weekend. You bring me good luck with women. But Freddy, before I speak to them, let's be clear: The tall one with the long shapely legs, the one with the miniskirt, she's mine. I'm taller than you. The curly one with the long hair in the turquoise tunic is yours. She looks nice too. Just so we're agreed."

Freddy, who had just gone on leave from his combat unit and was still in uniform, thought that the 'deal' was fair and appropriate. He felt lucky to be in female company that evening. After two weeks of hard training, he was certainly not picky and was willing to go along with the plan devised by his good friend. The girls facing them had no idea why the fancy car was on the pavement and what was happening inside with the two young men, who had already 'split' the girls between them.

Several minutes after the sudden halt, everything had gone according to Tommy's plan. With his sharp tongue and his personal charm, he left the two buxom young ladies no choice, no way of refusing his invitation to the party. He definitely didn't let them change his 'predetermined choice'. From the moment he first approached them, it was clear who would be dating whom, who was paired with whom.

Tommy never had any inhibitions, certainly not when it came to the opposite sex. He said: "This is my good friend Freddy and I am Tommy. I tried to rhyme but it didn't work this time". All four seemed at ease. The ensuing conversation left no doubt where the four would spend the evening, and of course who would date whom.

The party at Nicky's, the son of a top industrialist, was particularly successful and productive. It was the precursor of a lengthy friendship between Lily and Tommy, and a little less lengthy between Freddy and Evie.

Tommy was an impressive man – in his looks, his sense of business, and his communicative ability to endear himself to anyone he met.

Freddy was almost the absolute opposite, a quiet guy who left a strong impression. He was more thorough and reliable than his friend, who was inclined to make promises without necessarily following through. Tommy and Lily's friendship continued for two years, throughout her military service at an air force base in southern California, not far from Santa Barbara.

The party was also the beginning of an intimate friendship between Evie and Freddy. It lasted about 15 months and ended when Freddy completed his military service and moved to the East Coast to study at a Connecticut university where his uncle was a professor. During these 15 months, the two couples often spent time together at parties, trips, at the beach, and at concerts, accumulating many joint experiences.

* * *

Lily recovered from her reminiscing in the lecture hall. She barely survived the second half of the evening, a screening of the film 'Nostalgic drama'. She made a decision to 'act decisively' when the film ended. Exiting the hall, she watched Freddy, who was sitting in the next row. He went to the restroom. She followed him. She told her friends that she was going to the restroom. They waited for her at the exit. She planned to bump into him near the restroom, as though by chance.

Freddy was amazed when he saw her and said, both astonished and admiring: "Wow. Lily, right?! Lily from the Santa Barbara intersection, right?! Unbelievable…"

"Yes", answered Lily, acting surprised as well.

"Wow, Evie's Freddy. Evie's Freddy. I can't believe it".

In the circumstances, the two only spoke a few sentences. They exchanged telephone numbers at her suggestion, rapidly and efficiently. Unclear prospective developments were put into motion by this act, both good and bad.

He hastened to return to his wife and she to her friends, as though nothing had happened.

Freddy was amazed by the coincidence of their unexpected meeting. This was the first time that he had come to the lecture series with his wife, Tracy. The friend who usually attended the theatre with her was ill, and he had joined his wife at her request, after unsuccessfully attempting to convince her to offer the free ticket to another friend. Tracy had insisted that he come; she felt it was important that he, as her husband, join her at least once. This evening was a good opportunity.

Lily couldn't wait for the night to end. She called him quite early the next day on her way to work. Freddy was not surprised by her early phone call. They counted the hours, and then the minutes, until their meeting at the elegant café in a nearby town where Lily had suggested they meet that day at 4pm. Lily and Freddy were as excited as if this was the first date of two teenagers, or maybe an extramarital affair between two married people enjoying a romantic fling.

"I suggested that we meet because for many years I have been waiting to see you and to tell you a secret that involves both of us: What a pity that you and your friend Tommy unfairly chose to 'split' Evie and myself among you. That's how I saw it. The year or so that Tommy and I double-dated with you and my friend Evie was an ordeal for me. And it became harder the more I got to know you on our double dates. I f-a-n-t-a-s-i-z-e-d about you, even when it looked like I was flirting with your friend Tommy… The only reason I didn't end my friendship with Tommy was so that I could continue fantasizing about you on our frequent double dates. After you and Evie broke up, I only went on dating Tommy because he would not hear of me leaving and repeatedly managed to stop me."

Freddy was totally amazed. He could not believe it. He never thought that Lily had had such feelings for him. The young lady whom he had so desired – her femininity, her sexuality, and her playfulness combined with practical sense. The truth was that he remembered sometimes feeling jealous of Tommy for his girlfriend Lily. He never gave any hint of this, neither to Lily nor to anyone else…

Lily went on, noting his turmoil at the secrets she had revealed: "You see, last night when the lecture series focused on drama in films I felt that for me the real drama was seeing you in the lecture hall and revealing these secrets to you after so many years. Even then there were times when I wanted to tell you how much I wanted you, but I didn't want to do anything to hurt Evie, who was my best friend. I also didn't dare hurt Tommy, who was your best friend. So I realized that I would have to live with my fantasies, with no hope of realizing them…"

Freddy couldn't restrain himself and interrupted Lily's flow of revelations and emotions: "Do you know why Evie and I broke up?"

"Yes, I know. When Evie decided to break up with you she told me that she didn't feel that she loved you enough, that you weren't exactly who she imagined as the 'man of her life'. She appreciated you as a person, but not as her spouse, her boyfriend for life".

"Do you want to know the real truth?!" He didn't wait for her to answer and went on:

"The evening we broke up we went to a movie and I told Evie that if I hadn't been Tommy's best friend I would have liked to realize my fantasy with her friend Lily…"

Lily was astounded and felt that she had missed out in a big way. Freddy continued to amaze her with his revelations:

"Just before I got married in Boston, towards the end of my doctoral studies at the age of 31, Tracy, my intended, asked me whether I had ever really been in love with a woman. She knew that I had had quite a few steady girlfriends and girls I had dated for short lengths of time. I replied with confidence and told her that I had loved several girls, but only once was I really in love. Tracy asked me about the lucky girl and what had happened to her. I told her, confessed to her, that it was you, Lily. Yes, yes, you Lily; Lilush as Evie used to call you. But I told Tracy that it had been a virtual love affair, that only one side knew about it…"

The two asked the inquisitive waiter who stopped by their table for another number three margarita cocktail, with a rich Roquefort and pear salad. They shared the dish.

"What about you, Lily, how did you manage to retain your female charm even at our advanced age? I mean advanced compared to the past… Does anyone know of your love for me?"

"About twelve years ago I was at an evening auction in Las Vegas and someone hugged me from behind. It was Evie. She had put on a lot of weight, but retained the three features that had always been her special mark: her smile, her warmth, and her endless hugs. It was exciting to see her after so many years. She was newly divorced with two children, and she told me the story of her life since we separated. She had lived with her family for many years in Santa Anna, California, where she was married to a millionaire lawyer. She told me something that touched my heart: 'Lily, I had everything in life, but I had nothing, I didn't really love my husband who would do everything for me and gave me everything, love, money, support, and admiration.' And then she continued to amaze me: 'Too bad that I didn't tell you then how jealous I was of you, and that it was Tommy whom I loved. Maybe you would have switched places with me. We were such good friends.'"

Lily was very excited. She surprised herself and stretched her hand out to Freddy, softly stroking his fingers.

"How did you respond to this revelation?"

"With two words: Big miss. Sorry, three words: 'Double big miss'!..."

"Evie cried out 'What?! Wait a minute, Lilush, what do you mean by 'double'?..."

"This was the first and only time that I ever told my secret. I told her about our mutual missed opportunity."

Freddy was sweating from the tension and he asked the waitress for a napkin to mop the sweat from his face. A few seconds later Lily produced her next 'bombshell', as though the previous crazy events were not enough: "I am a divorced woman, and I now look my best. You see how I look as a woman over 50. And I have not advanced in age only. I am a valued employee of a prestigious academic institute; I have nearly reached the top. My three children are doing well and have left home. I have a nice house. I have almost everything I want aside from one thing. And you can provide it. I know, as you told me, that you are happily married to Tracy. I have no intention of trying to erode your good relationship. I only ask that you come home with me for one evening and help me put to rest a fantasy that has lasted many years. A one-time evening, not to be repeated. Sort of like a 'precise medical procedure'."

After three exciting hours, four cocktails, and one woman - his wife, who went to visit her parents for the night - Freddy agreed to Lily's request, although he admittedly had his qualms. He felt a mixture of emotions and thoughts that included fear, curiosity, nostalgia, adventure, conscience pangs, masculinity, and more than all an urge to realize a fantasy of his own. And this urge was the last straw that helped him decide.

"I agree, but only if for this one night I can call you by the name I have

whispered within me for years:
'Maxi Mini', be mine for one night..."

After that evening, which culminated in a special night, Lily's fantasy dissolved, disappeared, leaving no trace.
It left her in a state of tranquility. She enjoyed accessing dating websites and feeling desired once again. The 'procedure' was crowned by success and her fantasy ceased, leaving no residues, no inhibitions.

Fifteen magical fascinating months since Lily first began cruising the dating websites, she chose David of all her suitors, for a second, happy, and lengthy relationship.

Freddy managed to reach joyful fulfillment with his wife Tracy and his children Andy and Ella, chalking up another life experience, or rather: the experience of a lifetime...

The fate of Evie and Tommy, the two other members of the foursome, remains unknown...

'Even the past does not remain unchanged, especially when some focus on enhancing the past while others forget the past'.

20

The charming '60s

● ● ●

Jennifer Florin Baldwin, who had passed her fiftieth birthday, took another break, sipping from her glass of gin and inhaling the smoke from her cigarette. She repeated this ritual several times throughout an overcast evening in the fall of 2006. This dual act of drinking and drawing the smoke into her lungs served to define the separate blues tunes. She played each piece with the talent of a professional, and her deep melodious voice accompanied the soulful notes.

Her daughter Diana, a pretty 19 year old, listened to her mother's singing and playing from her post in the joint kitchen-and-living room, where she was washing dishes in the sink. As usual, Diana interrupted her beloved mother and asked her: "Mom, why are you so melancholic tonight?" She had just reached the end of 'All alone am I', a Sixties classic.

"Tonight I acutely feel the absence of your father George, my beloved husband and friend. Today is the 25th anniversary of the day we first met. I can remember how my gaze was drawn to him, of all the many people in the audience at the air force base, when I came on stage to perform before the pilots and other officers. For both of us it was love at first sight. Our wedding was quick, modest, and emotional. Every day since that terrible injury I fell in love with him, with Georgie, anew. Today I feel extremely tormented. I miss him, and that's why I've chosen tonight's sad repertoire, Diana my love. My sense of loneliness without my Georgie and my longing for him are intertwined, especially today, on the anniversary of our first meeting. And tonight this emotional turmoil is enhanced by memories of my career as a popular singer and pianist, interrupted by that accursed injury. Up to that time I had filled many night clubs specializing in blues and country music, particularly in Oklahoma but also in other southern cities."

Jennifer ended her tearful outburst. Once again, she placed her hands on the keyboard. But her only daughter, who together with Jennifer's memories and her piano encompassed her entire universe, said: "My dear mother, there is a time for singing and playing, and a time for talking and revealing…

Now please leave the piano stool and come hug me on the sofa. On this special day, tell me as much as you can about dad and about the two of you. For a long time you and I have been silent, keeping our thoughts to ourselves. We have hardly spoken of him and of your life together. But before you tell me about dad, I have an important question for you: Mom, how did you manage to keep your good looks over the years?…"

"One thing I've learned in life, my dear daughter, is that compliments are very good for you. Certainly in moments such as this. Thank you, Diana, for your complimentary words." She hugged her tightly and gave her a drawn-out kiss on the cheek.

"I too, mom, have learned something, although I'm still young, and it is that compliments are better than complaints. Compliments strengthen and complaints weaken…"

"That's right, my daughter, you're right on the mark, as usual. I'm not surprised that you are an outstanding student. What else did you want to ask?"

"What did dad like, how did he live, what type of music, dancing, culture, fashion, literature, movies… To what was he most attached? I want to know more about his favorite things, aside from the love of his life, about whom I know everything… Can you repeat what you have already told me about dad…?"

"Tonight I'll tell you, Diana, a lot of the things you have asked about… But I suggest that after I finish you check out websites on the Sixties. Dad was a real Sixties' freak. His life was a perfect reflection of that period, one he loved so much. You can access those sites and join forums that discuss the era that dad lived every day, even when commanding his squadron in the early eighties". Jennifer told Diana about George, their husband

and father. She even told her that her father had named her for a famous Sixties song of his contemporary idol, Canadian singer Paul Anka. This was the first time that Diana had heard the reason for her given name, to which she had always felt particularly attached. Jennifer felt very relieved at having opened up to her daughter and at the opportunity to illuminate other aspects in the personality of her late husband, whom she had so admired.

Until this day, even on this intimate evening between the two of them, she had not told her daughter that George had shot himself in the head when Diana was two years old. He did it because he did not want the child to see her father in a wheelchair. He didn't want to embarrass his beloved daughter. She had lied to Diana and told her that her father had been hit by a stray bullet while out hunting. Diana knew that her father had been wounded a year after she was born but did not know that he had been confined to a wheelchair. Her mother had made sure to conceal this fact from her.

* * *

One of the websites, 'Classics of the sixties', attracted Diana most of all. She began a conversation with a young man named Roy from a distant unknown country, who happened to be logged onto the site. He too was interested in the Sixties, for a very unusual reason… completely unlike Diana's.

Roy Feldman from Ramat Hasharon was an outstanding student of sociology and anthropology at his university. It was 1am in Israel and he was bent over his computer, immersed in his activities. He was the only one at home. His mother Muriel had gone skiing in the French Alps with friends. His sister was at her army base. His father had told him that morning that he would return late at night after having dinner with his guests from overseas.

The main entrance to the villa opened and Gidi, Roy's father, a tall man with a well-toned body, entered the house. He promptly headed for his son's welcoming and well-lit room. Roy knew that his parents' relationship had deteriorated in recent years. From the beginning, their marriage had known many crises and disputes. His mother's European mentality, coming as she did from Belgium, clashed with his father's earthiness as a former kibbutz member. She had no strong roots in Israel. She did not feel an authentic Israeli and remained very close to her family and friends in Belgium. The contrast between their attitudes was obvious. Roy suspected that his father had been having an affair with another woman for the past two years. And he was right.

The relationship between Roy and his father was cool. The father expressed little interest in his son's life. They had many disagreements. Even their political views were incompatible. The son usually took his mother's side in his parents' conflicts, as he saw her as the victim. Lately his younger sister, Noa the soldier, often spoke to him of trying to improve his relationship with his father. She herself was more neutral and told her brother that their mother was no less at fault for their situation, which naturally also had an impact on the lives of the children. Roy listened attentively to his sister's arguments. He loved her and admired her practical sense.

As a result of these conversations he decided to change his attitude to his father and to make a gesture which, he hoped, would help improve their relationship.
"Hi, Roy, good night," Gidi said to his son from the entrance to his room.
"I see that you're still at your studies so late at night…"
"The truth is that this time I'm actually occupied with your hobby… in fact, your big love."
Gidi, who knew that his son usually took his mother's side, and that his relationship with his father was reserved and suspicious, was alarmed and afraid that his son had found out about his affair with a fairly well known divorcee. Maybe he even knew from where he was returning so late at night, with his wife away in Europe. And maybe, the father feared in those moments of inner embarrassment mixed with anxiety, his son was surfing the web and gathering information about the woman…
"'The love of my life', what do you mean?"
And then Roy surprised his father, who responded with a sigh of relief:
"I'm finding out about something that you really love and that we never supported. I mean your endless love for anything related to the Sixties. So I decided to do something about it. I will write my thesis in sociology on this period, to which you feel so connected. It is in your honor, dad. I will examine the thesis that the Sixties was the most influential decade in the past century, with its effect on consumer culture, musical styles, and mass media."

Gidi the father was astounded and very happy at Roy's words. Such an unexpected statement by his son was outstanding, with its surprising and honest desire to strengthen their ties. He had waited and hoped for this moment for so long. He had even spent dozens of sessions with a well known psychologist, consulting with him on how to improve his relationship with his son. Until tonight nothing had done the trick. And now it had arrived, so surprisingly, now of all times, when his wife – Roy's mother – was abroad.

"I'd be glad to help you with anything you need for your paper…" He couldn't and didn't want to conceal his excitement. "I'll tell you about contemporary influential events in Israel and in the world. I'll tell you about interesting personal experiences that will reflect insights from that time. I will help you analyze the songs, male and female singers, and groups that affected the musical styles of the following decades… Oh, I have a great idea. I'll introduce you to the directors of the global firm 'Trends Plus'. They'll give you lots of material for your paper. They provide us and other publicity firms in the world with material to help develop nostalgic marketing and advertising campaigns targeting mainly, but not only, top 'golden age' audiences. They have lots of interesting information on the Sixties…"

Roy and Gidi hugged each other, something they had not done in a long time.

In these uplifting moments, it seemed that Roy's nostalgic thesis, a gesture to his father, would indeed become a stable rehabilitating bridge in their relationship.

The online chats between Diana in St. Louis, Missouri, and Roy in Ramat Hasharon, Israel, became gradually more frequent and daring. At first they exchanged lots of information on other Sixties' websites as well as on books, films, television series on the period. But over the three months of their relationship they developed intimate conversations. They exchanged photographs, e-mails expressing their intimacy, and loving and passionate messages. They planned to meet in the near future. Roy even had a practical idea on how to consummate their desire, their passion…

In their conversations the two eager youngsters expressed constant amazement at their unusual reasons for visiting websites on issues so far from their world, separated from them by decades, typical of their parents' era. She wanted to know more about her father's life, whom she had not known. He wanted to improve and enhance his relationship with his own father.

Diana told Roy how the combat plane flown by her father in a training sortie had crashed, and about the serious injury that had brought calamity upon their family. She told him that her mother had said that a short while after being wounded her father died 'in tragic circumstances', in her words. She told him about her mother's frequent depressions, and about the alcohol to which she had become quite addicted.

Diana excitedly followed the improved relationship between Roy and his father, a product of Roy's thesis on the Sixties. After all, this was the reason that she herself had been caught up on the web in an affair with a distant young man. Roy shared with her the contents of his paper and his father's contribution.

Diana told him in a conversation on Skype, at night in her time zone, that she had told her mother about her online romance with an Israeli, and had asked her if she knew anything about 'that distant tiny country'. Diana's mother smiled and immediately began to play the music to the eternal hit 'Those were the days' on the piano. Playing this nostalgic music, she told her daughter that in 1973 she had flown to Israel with a group of young Baptist Christians from the southern US to offer their help at the conclusion of a tormenting war. They volunteered to help out at packing factories, greenhouses, orchards, hospitals, and at places called 'kibbutzim' where people lived a communal life.

Roy told Diana that his father had told him that during that same war, when her mother had come to volunteer in Israel, his father had been a combat officer living on a kibbutz in southern Israel. There were many volunteers at the kibbutz, working in agriculture, with the cows and chickens, and also studying the local language in classes called 'ulpan'… "Hebrew," Diana interrupted him. "My mother told me about it… What an incredible coincidence…"

An hour later she called Roy again on Skype, all aflutter: "My mother would like to know your father's given name. She admitted that at the time, when she volunteered in your country, she had a short affair with a handsome combat officer. Maybe your father knows him, and who knows

– maybe it was him, and we both have a half-brother, you through your father and me through my mother… and then we won't be able to be together when we meet. What will we do?!" Diana liked to fool around in her conversations with him. She enjoyed it. It was her way of expressing her joy at their strong virtual connection.

In their conversations Roy enjoyed their sense of humor and witticisms, now more than ever. "My father's given name is Gideon, but everyone calls him 'Gidi'… In our recent conversations he told me about his life in the sixties, and even later until he married my mother, that he had a short and passionate relationship with a volunteer at his kibbutz right after the war. I asked him for details. He thought about it and said that he seemed to remember that she came from the southern US, but not from Missouri, he thinks it was Oklahoma. I mentioned your mother's name, Jennifer, but dad said that he was certain that was not her name. So we have nothing to worry about… there's no chance that we have a half-brother somewhere out there…"
"You've convinced me. So when will we meet here and realize our love? We've been together but not together for several months now. I tell all my suitors at college, and there are quite a few, that I have a boyfriend. I've just finished the semester with outstanding grades and that is good reason to celebrate, together with your thesis and your 'excellent' grade."

"I'll check with dad exactly when he's planning on going to the conference in Chicago. He wants me to come with him and in fact he has already invited me. From there I will continue to you in St. Louis. I'll try to convince him to come with me. He and your mother can reminisce about the war in which both of them were involved, she as a volunteer and he as a soldier. And we, their descendants, will continue to focus on our love.

Muriel, Roy's mother, returned from her ski vacation in Europe, one that had lasted longer than anticipated.

When she returned she asked her husband Gidi for a divorce. The children were grown and in any case they had not been intimate for quite a long time. She told him in all honesty that she had met a widowed Belgian childhood friend at the ski club in the Alps and that she felt he was the right man for her now. She also said that she had known for quite a while that Gidi was being unfaithful to her but had turned a blind eye to avoid rocking the boat and hurting their sensitive children. She had waited until their daughter Noa enlisted in the army.

"Come, Gidi, let's do the right and fair thing for us and for the children we love and get a proper divorce as soon as possible. We are both in good shape. You can have a serious relationship with your girlfriend Sherry. I can be true to my European mentality with no qualms and without your reproaches. We will always remain the loving parents of our wonderful children. I was glad to hear from Roy about your budding relationship. I too will strengthen my relationship with Noa, whom I have neglected somewhat recently, and I will take her on a vacation from the army at her beloved grandparents' in Antwerp."
The two promptly and civilly agreed on the terms of their divorce.

Two weeks later Muriel and Gidi signed a divorce agreement at their lawyer's, a joint acquaintance specializing in family matters, to their mutual satisfaction.
Then they gathered their children and told them of the developments. Their son and daughter were not surprised by the divorce.

As a 'divorce present' the daughter Noa received a ticket to Belgium from her mother, with an open invitation for both of them to tour Europe for a week. This was part of Muriel's attempt to improve her relationship with her daughter. The son Roy also received a nice present from his father, a tempting offer to join him for a conference on 'advertising and the internet' in Chicago. The 'cherry' was the added leg of the trip to visit his beloved Diana at her home in Missouri, in a pleasant suburb of St. Louis.
Roy easily convinced his newly divorced father to come with him and visit Diana and her mother Jennifer.

The encounter in southern St. Louis between the two pairs, the visiting son and father from Ramat Hasharon and the hosts, the daughter Diana and the mother Jennifer, was amazing and touching. Once the door opened the two young people hugged each other at length. After a short time in the living room, Roy and Diana went upstairs to her room and reemerged only the next afternoon, 16 hours later. They realized all their fantasies from the past four months, leaving nothing to their imagination.

The older two remained in the living room, in a daze. Jennifer recovered after several minutes, sat down by the piano and played and sang 'Cheek to cheek'. Gidi felt himself tremble, a feeling that spread to his entire body. He suddenly remembered how much he had loved this song, one that she had sung and played for him when they stole into the kibbutz culture room to the only piano.

Thirty three years came to an end... the two had no more doubts...
Gidi and Diana reminisced about their short passionate affair on his kibbutz right after the Yom Kippur war, when she had volunteered to work in the chicken coop and studied Hebrew at the ulpan. He was a combat commander, a good looking man. She was a girl from Oklahoma, full of life, and she admitted to him that in Israel she had introduced herself to everyone, and to him and the group of Baptist volunteers as well, by her middle name, Florin. No one knew her as Jennifer, not even Gidi.
"And that's exactly what I remembered about you, that your name was Florin and not Jennifer. You were like a flower to me, and just as I remembered you were from Oklahoma, not from Missouri. Now everything's clear... and I feel better about my memory..."

Only one of the two couples in the house in the suburb of St. Louis made love that day, repeatedly.
The two young people, crazily in love, had an intensely physical experience, while Gidi remained true to his girlfriend Sherry, with whom he had been unfaithful to his wife for two years, and Jennifer remained loyal to Georgie, her late husband.

In 2013 the readers can be told of the following facts and developments...

Roy and Diana are living happily in a pleasant residential area in central Israel. They have a wonderful family.

Pianist and singer Jennifer Florin Baldwin had an incredible comeback. She performs very successfully almost every evening at the high class music club 'Return to Joy' using her middle name, Florin, not far from her daughter Diana, her son-in-law Roy, and her grandchildren, four year old Ben and two year old Noga. This is the family that reawakened her happiness. She combines many rhythmic and happy rock and swing songs in her performances, together with blues ballads.

Each of Roy's parents found happiness with their new spouses. His father with Sherry, a celebrated media personage. His mother with Charles the Belgian, a successful diamond trader.

Incidentally, from time to time they all come to the 'Return to joy' club to listen to the wonderful singer Florin, or Jennifer Florin Baldwin, the 'one and only'…

'Compliments strengthen those who give them': Be generous with your support (when appropriate).
It is good for you too!

21

A rare wartime encounter

● ● ●

Hilik had been fortunate in those minutes, when terrible fire was aimed at his small military unit on the last day of the festival of Simhat Torah, a short two hours before the ceasefire was to come into effect at 6pm.

His entire face was bloody, his eyes almost covered in blood. His left arm and right leg had also been hit by shrapnel from the Syrian shells. This combination of serious injuries and bleeding with a sense of being 'fortunate' seemed strange, if not absurd. It reflected the relativity of life and its fragility. Only a short while ago, Hilik and his friends had had a conversation about the role of fate in life in the command car.

His good friend Shayke, an observant Jew, had passionately defended his viewpoint whereby 'everything is determined from above', in his words.

Now, less than an hour after the conversation on fate between the five reserve soldiers in the armored car, Shayke, a good guy, was no longer alive.

Less than half a meter from his charred corpse, officer Meir, who had been persistent in his view that 'You are the master of your destiny', lay mortally wounded. The argument had been interrupted when the first shells landed, a last desperate Syrian attempt to improve their position.

Tragically, after the conversation about fate in life, fate had been so cruel to their unit.

Of the five soldiers who had been together at the time of the bombardment three had been hit:

Shayke was killed, Meir was injured and was barely alive. Gabi and Shalom miraculously remained physically untouched, but in time it would become clear that their mental scars, in the form of combat shock, would remain with them for years to come. The young soldier Hilik, standing between the dead and the seriously injured, was in relatively 'good' shape, with injuries that in military jargon were defined as 'medium'. For the first time in his life Hilik was happy to be 'medium' at something. Being medium was something that he had always abhorred: at work, in school, in friendships, and in life.

Two helicopters of the medical corps landed next to the small military unit. Hilik did not know what had happened to the two friends who had been with him. All three had been hit by the same shell.

The soldier diagnosed as having 'medium injuries' was dazed. He was semi-conscious.

The first medic, a Yemenite by descent, left the helicopter and ran over to Hilik who had lost lots of blood. A second medic approached the mortally wounded man. The two medics determined that the third man injured was dead and that the two wounded must be tended to immediately in the field. They split up. The short swarthy man focused on Hilik. He managed to stem most of the bleeding fairly quickly. Holding the hand that had not been injured he asked: "What's your name, dear boy?" The question was loaded with emotion. It was a way of checking a soldier's state of consciousness after an injury more than something formal the medic must know about a wounded man as part of the procedures of medical care and evacuation.

The wounded man heard the question and the medic took it as a good sign. He whispered "Yehiel Melman". The medic did not understand what was going on. How did the man know his name? He held both of the soldier's hands, feeling a special connection to him from the moment they had met beyond the medic-patient relationship …

"What's y-o-u-r name?!" He emphasized the word 'your'. With his remaining strength the wounded man repeated his previous answer: "Yehiel Melman".

The Yemenite medic with the expansive soul and wide heart confirmed with officer Gabi, who had not been hit in the bombardment, that this was indeed the injured man's name. What an unbelievable coincidence. And these were not common Israeli names, like Moshe Cohen or Avi Levy. He turned to the officer and the wounded man, whose eyes were half open and half closed, and said excitedly and tearfully: "Would you believe it, Yehiel Melman the wounded cared for by Yehiel Melman the medic. But we are so different...". Several minutes later, when they were in the helicopter, he couldn't get over his amazement at the fact that in such circumstances he had met a man with the same name as his, for the first time in his 23 and a half years. They even shared the nickname 'Hilik'.

The care provided at the Poriya hospital in Tiberias was extremely devoted. A complex operation to remove shrapnel from Hilik's eye went well and the three doctors who performed the procedure were able to tell the injured reserve soldier, his parents and girlfriend waiting outside the operating room, that he would regain all his sight. His injured hand was also treated and it healed.

Every two or three days, in between his assignments, the medic with the Yemenite appearance came to visit the wounded man to whom he had become attached. Hilik recovered and recuperated, and conscious of the mystical coincidence he shared the incredible story with all his visitors at the hospital. His sister Hedva said to him: "Maybe you arranged for the injury only so that we could all enjoy this fantastic story..." Hedva, who was the editor of her school newspaper, always uttered such statements. This time her morbid sense of humor was a source of smiles around the patient's bed.
When the commander of the brigade to which his unit had been annexed came to tell him that his two friends, Shayke and Meir, who had been standing next to him when they were attacked, were no longer alive, he remembered the statement 'It is all from above'. It suddenly received a completely different meaning. Even the argument about fate in the armored car seemed to belong to the distant past. Certainly not something that had been said a minute or two before he had been wounded. He felt that the 'above' had chosen only him of the three to remain alive. The battle for Meir's life had been lost as he was taken off the evacuating chopper.
The 'everything from above' had also chosen to send Hilik Melman to him, leaving at least two men with that name among the living.

Hilik's recovery was amazing and two weeks after arriving at the hospital he was transferred to a military convalescence home in Acre.
Hilik the medic no longer came to visit him. He returned home from reserve duty and was busy helping his family in the city of Rehovot. He felt that

his task had been completed when he saw Hilik recovering quickly, with only a small scar under his eye to remind him of the war. Rehovot, where he lived and worked, was quite a distance from Acre, where the soldier was recuperating. Soldier Hilik's home in Haifa was almost as far.

In their last encounter, recovering Hilik had given Hilik the medic a book written by his father, describing the history of his family during the Holocaust in Europe. The book carried a heartfelt dedication on its first page:

"Dear Hilik, I owe you a lot, so much. Someone from 'above' will certainly see that we meet again, unexpectedly, and this time I hope that it will be in different circumstances, joyful ones. I will never forget what you did for me..."

The two hugged each other goodbye. Soldier Hilik's family and the medical staff, who had fallen in love with both Hiliks, were no less excited than the patient and the medic who found it hard to take their leave of each other.

Finally they let go and proceeded to their post-war lives.

They were both young reserve soldiers and their lives were only beginning, urging them to each take his chosen course.

But their memories returned to haunt both of them at least for the first year after the war. Sometimes they appeared in dreams and sometimes while awake, retaining a dreamlike quality.

It took a year, maybe a little more, before the incredible incident with its rare and unbelievable coincidence was repressed, pushed into a distant part of their memory.

Both Melmans married several years later, had families, and often told people close to them about what had happened to them during the war. Hilik the medic cherished the book he had received from Hilik the patient with its dedication. He could not remember ever receiving a dearer present. To be exact, he knew that he never had. He was skeptical whether anything ever dedicated to him would excite him like the book he received at the hospital when saying goodbye to the man he had saved.

The years went by relatively quickly. There was a difference of only one number separating the year of the war, when fate had brought them together so strangely, and the current year. Then again, maybe this fate was indeed part of the package labeled 'Everything is from above'. The number 9 had replaced the 7. Twenty years had passed since that war, since that incredible incident. It was now the same season again, and as before, the autumn winds were blowing.

But before we get to this special day that arrived unbidden, let's retrace our steps…

About five years earlier, Hilik, once the patient, told his story at a friend's house. A producer of a popular television program, 'Our incredible life', listened to the story and was astounded by it and by the storyteller. The well known producer, who just happened to be there, promptly suggested that Hilik tell his story at her next program, marking the 15th anniversary of the war.

Hilik politely rejected her proposal, not giving in to the demands of most of those present who said: "Hilik, what a story!" He claimed that the experience was too intimate and that he would like to keep it to himself and tell it only in small forums, as he had done that night. From that night on memories of the injury, the operations, his recovery, and above all of the dedicated medic who rescued him, began to resurface. Thus, from time to time, he would think of the 'other' Hilik Melman, and ask himself curiously, "I wonder what happened to him?" This query arose anew every fall since the encounter with the television producer at the home of his friend.

All in all, aside from occasional problems, the last 20 years since the war had been good for both Melmans, each in his own way, each with his own expectations, and they were both happy in their own ways.

The former patient had done well and was appointed assistant director of a surgical department at a prominent hospital. In the hospital he established a company that invested in the development of innovative methods and means of performing operations in different medical domains. The start-up took off and his innovative developments attained global success. His work managing the start-up company involved much traveling by Professor Yehiel (Hilik) Melman.

The smart successful professor believed in paying others full personal attention. He himself would come to the airport in his car to pick up his guests, take them to their hotel, have a drink with them in the lobby, ask about their flight, and sometimes, if the circumstances were right, he would invite his guests on the day of their arrival to a meal at an authentic Israeli restaurant, or even at his home.

He would always recite to his medical staff – doctors and workers of all ranks and in his firm as well, the motto that shaped his attitude to life:

'In a world of output and input,
Personal attention more than all
Is the most important…
And the most worthwhile!'

He never said that he himself had also thought up and written this sentence. Sometimes he wondered to what degree the incredible encounter with the medic had contributed, whether consciously or not, to his adoption and application of this approach.

The American Jeff Randal was Hilik's closest confidante in the medical firm that he ran for the hospital. Officially, Prof. Melman was the Chairman of the Board of Directors. In practice, he was its living spirit: in charge of anything that had to do with initiatives, development, marketing, and general management. Aside from finances, which were his weak side. Dr. Jeff Randal raised capital for Prof. Melman all over the world. Over the last three years they had become close friends.

Prof. Melman loved Dr. Randal's special humor, always combined with lessons for life. Jeff had been blessed with a good sense of humor, but was also thoughtful, and sometimes had creative ideas that contributed to the development of the company. Yes, even that. Maybe, Hilik thought to himself whenever he met his close friend, it was thanks to his friend, who had attained a rare academic rank in the form of three PhDs: in philosophy, Far East studies, and business administration. Jeff always emphasized that this was the right order to mention his degrees.

One morning, when Prof. Melman was eagerly and happily anticipating his afternoon trip to welcome his guest at the airport, a problem arose with his car's brakes. He left the car at the garage and decided that for a change he would take a cab to the airport and back. The professor didn't even think of taking another car from the hospital or from the director of his start-up company. Of course, the option of asking his guest to take a cab to his hotel in Tel Aviv did not arise. He was excited to welcome his friend Jeff.

The encounter between the two at the arrival hall of the airport was warm and hearty as usual. "How is your new car?" asked the guest. "In the garage", answered his host, and added "It's an opportunity to travel by cab like two tourists in my own country. I would also like to see what it's like to take a cab incognito."

"And it will give me a chance to tell you a great Jewish joke about a cab driver, one that I heard at a cocktail party in Kansas two days ago. But first, how are Ariella and the kids?"

"Everyone's fine, thank God. And how is your family, Jeff?"

"Good, we're happy. Juliette sends you her regards and Barbara's doing well."

Their designated cab had disappeared when its driver heard the next couple in line ask for a cab to Naharia. The driver preferred to 'catch' the larger fare.

Prof. Melman and his guest had no problem taking the next cab, as the previous driver had been smoking a cigarette. They preferred to take another cab, with no cigarette smoke. And that's what happened. They spared the driver the need to open the boot, as the guest who had come for two days had only a small trolley that he placed on the seat beside him.

"So how does the joke go, Jeff?"

"Three Jewish women over 70, all yiddishe mamas, meet at the end of a lecture on seniors in New York. Each one tells the others about herself. The first one says: 'My name is Hilda, and the first thing I want to tell you is that I have an only son named Asher, and you know how proud I am of my son, he's the best doctor in New York.'

The second woman felt that she 'had to take up the maternal gauntlet.'

'And I am Sarah, and I have an only son as well, and he makes me very happy: Aharon is an advocate, the richest lawyer in New York.'

The two looked at the third, who seemed the best dressed. She took a deep breath, took another sip of her tea, and turned to the two women:

'Now it's my turn. My name is Feigele Zeitlin. My only son Jeffrey is loving and devoted. His profession?! He's a cab driver...'

Her two acquaintances were shocked. The mother of a cab driver in New York was no friend of theirs. Feigele noticed their discomfort and said: 'There's another thing that I'd like to tell you about my son: he's gay, homosexual....' The two other women immediately paid their bill, leaving a generous tip on the table, nodded to her with reserve and fled the café. Feigele ran after them begging: 'One minute, I'm proud of Jeffrey too...' Astounded, they stopped and turned to Feigele curiously, thinking that maybe he's also an artist, a musician, or proficient at some occupation or hobby in addition to simply being a cab driver... 'My Jeffrey has two boyfriends… one is the best doctor in New York, and the second is the richest lawyer in New York…!'"

Hilik and his visitor Jeff didn't know whether the driver was listening and had understood the joke. Prof. Melman burst out laughing and had just said: "She sure got them there, Jeff…" when he was suddenly interrupted by the driver who turned around, looked straight at him, and said: "Excuse me, sir, aren't you the soldier from…"

And boom! The moment the driver looked away there was a powerful crash. A motorcyclist overtaking the cab had wildly crashed into it's front end.

Hilik, the cab driver from Rehovot, didn't have a chance to finish his sentence. He only had time to reach the word 'from' and was cut off before the next words: 'the Yom Kippur war'…

Hilik the driver lay in the road. His face was bloodied.

The two passengers, Prof. Melman and his guest, jumped out, and the expert professor resuscitated the driver and managed to save his life.

Several minutes later the three were in an ambulance taking the injured man to the hospital.

Next to the cab's license and insurance records lay the book 'The incredible story of my family in the Holocaust' by Shmuel Melman.

On the second page of the book was a dedication written on November 8, 1973.

The injured cab driver was the former medic, and the professor was the wounded soldier. The man he was with at the hospital was the same man who had received from him, now a professor, this book 20 years ago, as a gesture in return for saving his own life.

Today, to his regret, he had the opportunity to repay the man who had saved his life…

Jeff Randal clapped his hands and asked his friend the professor: Is this the 'Everything from above' guy you told me about who saved your life during the war?!"

"Yes, yes, this is that precious fabulous person from my story. This is the man from whom I will never again become separated.

This time it's not only 'Everything from above'. This time it's a 'sign from above'…"

Jeff Randal from the United States hugged the professor and the injured cab driver, both of the same name, and muttered in amazement: "A story like this can happen only in Israel…"

Real giving benefits the giver. It is usually repaid with 'interest', unexpectedly and unintentionally.

22

A wonderful acquaintance in Prague

• • •

That evening the famous Black Theater of Prague was featuring the popular show Jazz Man. Isaac sat restlessly beside his elegant wife, waiting impatiently for the show to begin. At the same time, an impressive man of about 40 took his seat to their right and greeted them politely. His 'good evening' was uttered in English with a heavy Jewish-American accent, leaving the two in no doubt as to his faith and nationality.

"You speak English?!" Isaac asked the man in English. This was in fact a rhetorical question to which he and his wife already knew the answer.

"Yes," answered the pleasant man with a smile, surprised to find theater mates far from home. "My name is Yisrael, and I'm from New York."

"This is my wife Lillian and I'm Yitzhak, or Isaac. We're from Miami. Can I ask you what you're doing in Prague in such cold weather?"

"Yes, I'll tell you, certainly. I'm a lawyer representing customers in the matter of property in the Jewish Quarter here, property that belonged to their parents until the war."

"Would you like to guess why we've come to the Czech Republic in this wintry weather…? I'll give you as many guesses as you'd like… I'll stop you when you guess right, or when you run out of guesses, and then… I'll tell you. Whatever happens first. If you guess right we'll invite you out for a good hard cider at a beautiful café bar on the river. Actually, we'll

invite you even if you don't guess right. For you it's a sure thing. Deal?!..."
"As a lawyer," Isaac continued in a playful humorous tone, "I have to warn you that it's a tough guess. At the wonderful café with a view of the castle on the hill I'll tell you why I came to Prague yesterday with my wife, or indeed to the Czech Republic…"
"Isaac", Lillian interrupted him, "the show's starting. At the intermission, or later on at the café, Yisrael will try to guess, and then you'll have enough time to tell your whole story at length".

Yisrael, a pleasant man, felt fortunate tonight. After a tiring day at a law and notary office, dealing with the exhausting bureaucracy, he had now received for the price of one ticket both a show that he longed to see and also companions for the evening, as well as an interesting story. He himself had always been known among his acquaintances as an inquisitive man and a story lover. Even his colleagues in his New York office knew of this love, at times interpreted as a strength and at others a weakness. The ability to listen patiently to his clients' stories was in itself usually an advantage and ensured good communication with them. But then again, his tendency to draw out his stories in court was sometimes to his disadvantage as it tired the judges, or at least some of them.
Speaking of stories, when the show began he remembered reading something that he had liked:

'What has changed from the mythical era of bygone days to the current technological generation?!...
In the mythical era stories gave one gratification, and in the technological era gratification is the entire story!'

The charm of the show Jazz Man, featured for decades at the official distinguished Laterna Magica theater, had not waned and it remained as enchanting and classic as ever. Unsurprisingly, the Black Theater genre was one of the notable features of beautiful Prague with its creative unique culture, attracting millions of tourists annually in all seasons.

Throughout the acts and stunts of the actors, illuminated by neon lights that created magnificent fascinating moving pictures and compositions on stage, the thoughts of Isaac Goldman and Yisrael Abrams were elsewhere. The former constantly tried to imagine the special encounter that would take place the next night at a distant border town situated between Slovakia and the Ukraine, for which he had come all the way here with his wife and tomorrow they would travel there. This is what he would tell the man to his right whom he had just met, at the café. At the same time Yisrael was thinking to himself, what could be a more special and incredible reason than his own visit to Prague. He had come here for two or three weeks for a special purpose, to recover historical and sentimental property for his clients, the son and daughter of Holocaust victims.

The intermission was too short for Isaac's special story that he wished to share with someone else in addition to his wife. Isaac Goldman had good intuition that had helped him rise and grow from a little boy who had been orphaned, hidden, and smuggled, to a successful man, popular among all his acquaintances. They didn't always understand his sense of humor, but they did enjoy his company. Isaac brought glasses of sparkling white wine and peanuts from the bar for the three of them. They toasted each other and Isaac said to the nice lawyer, "This is the beginning of a friendship that began at the theater and will continue in life, and this is also only the introduction to the story that you will hear at the café."

Isaac Goldman was a financial success, in relative terms, and he had made a living for himself and his family through hard work and ingenuity in the wood and paper business. He was proud of his family, his two successful grown-up children, his eldest daughter Julia and his son Nathan, as well as his wife Lillian, born in Germany, whom he loved every day anew. His noble dog Shadow was an inseparable part of the family. He longed to be called 'Grandpa Isaac' but the children were in no hurry, particularly Julia the eldest who was 32 and divorced.
"Only when you'll be a mother will I consider you both perfect and whole," said Isaac to his daughter. She, who was a real achiever and pretty, admired her father and answered him on more than one occasion: "Dear father, don't worry about me. I'll take care of myself and you focus on what occupies you, and on what is most important in your life... I'm a big girl. One day I'll be a mother. You know that I love children. Mother and you will be contented grandparents, I promise."

Isaac had found more time to devote to his children in recent years, despite their busy lives, as well as to his volunteer work in various social organizations. His life was full of good things. He was happy with the course he had chosen and with his life. Beyond his strong desire to be a grandfather, the one thing he yearned for was what he was about to tell

Yisrael. It was indeed the matter that had occupied him throughout his adult life more than any. He was preoccupied and annoyed that he had not yet managed to figure out his 'life story'. In recent years, as the rate of his work and business had gradually slowed, his longing to solve the question, the problem, intermixed with almost all aspects of his life, only became more pressing. In the last year this problem had been bothering him more and more, both in his thoughts and in his activities. As part of the actions he took he had arrived the night before in the Czech Republic and tomorrow he would travel to Slovakia with his wife.

Isaac Goldman was the son of Gita and Berl who were killed in the Holocaust with his two brothers and sister in the Ukraine. When he was 3 years old his entire family had been murdered by the Eizensgruppen, a unit of the Nazis and their Ukraine collaborators. He, Isaac, was fortunate, and his life was saved. As a child he heard from a distant acquaintance who later passed away that his neighbors had managed to hide and save him. The acquaintance hadn't really known his family, but had heard the story in vague terms. Isaac did not remember his parents and his 3 older siblings who were buried in a mass grave.

He longed to find his rescuers, or at least one of them. He had an intense inner longing to meet them, to thank them for being alive and for having a family. He yearned for any description of his parents, his two brothers and sister.

Money, time, and daring posed no barrier or limitation for him. He approached different people in the US and overseas to help him locate links and find pieces of information, either voluntarily or for payment, sometimes even large sums. In this way he had reached the city of Rovno in the Ukraine two months ago, hoping to find his saviors or their descendants. In Rovno he found a distant acquaintance who mentioned a Ukrainian family that was living in Prague and gave him rumored information about his family. He said that Isaac was the son of a teacher in a heder, a Jewish nursery school. His father had known distant relatives of Isaac's parents. They were living in Prague. Last night, right after he and his wife Lillian landed, they met with an elderly couple of about 90 and Isaac conversed with them through a translator. They told him that the man who had known his family was now living in a small village in Slovakia, near the border with the Ukraine.

Verbal communication with the couple was difficult. They were not completely lucid. He managed to elicit pieces of information that led him to take a gamble and decide to travel tomorrow with a translator to the remote village in Slovakia. A contact on his behalf informed the family of the elderly man in the border town, who had passed the age of 90, and coordinated Isaac's arrival there with his wife.

Isaac felt a deep need that night to tell this story to a stranger who would be attentive and empathic. Yisrael, the lawyer from New York, whom he had met at the theater in the early show two and a half hours ago, was the right person. He listened eagerly to every word. The desire to tell matched the passion to listen. It was a winning encounter. The timing of their meeting was perfect.

As the story progressed Yisrael became even more enthralled. Once, when he saw Isaac wipe away a tear with a slight shiver of excitement, he interrupted the flow of his story and told him that "the show the three of us saw together tonight was very symbolic... Most of the stage was dark, and neons flashed, creating the story of the 'jazz man'...". "This", continued Yisrael excitedly, "was also true of that dark period, there were some flashes of light in the form of those Righteous among the Nations whose story you are telling me."

This idea, voiced by Yisrael, captured the imagination of the couple with whom he was spending this exciting evening. Only thirty minutes ago, when they arrived at the charming Danube Tastes café on the river with a view of the impressive castle on the hill, Yisrael had 'failed' the 'test of possible reasons'. He tried to guess the reason for the couple's visit, whether tourism, medicine and therapies, various types of business, a visit to a grave or graves of relatives, matters of inheritance, political or social contacts, and even suggested that they had come to visit a son or daughter studying in the Czech Republic. None of the lawyer's guesses hit the mark.

As agreed at the theater, once Yisrael reached the end of his suggestions, albeit with no success, Isaac began his fascinating story. For over an hour the curious lawyer eagerly listened to the words of the older man.

Isaac and Lillian would not let Yisrael pay the bill, or at least cover his part of the tasty meal of pies, quiches, and wine they had ordered at the restaurant.

They separated and agreed to meet at the café in two days' time. Then Isaac would tell Yisrael what had happened at the meeting in the Slovakian border town...

The cab trip to the remote town, with Jan the affable translator and the couple's video camera, was a long one and took about four and a half hours. The son of the elderly man, with whom the meeting had been coordinated, told them that his father did not remember many details of the war years, which were by now about sixty years in the past. But when he had been lucid he had spoken of hearing that his cousin had saved a Jewish boy, risking his own family to do so. The son of the elderly Ukrainian, now speaking for his father, was not in touch with this maternal cousin. But he thought that the cousin had lived in Prague, and once or twice he had read in the newspaper that a son of the cousin's relative is a successful lawyer. He told Isaac his name, Advocate Peter Jankolovski, but knew nothing else about him. The meeting was less successful than Isaac had anticipated, but still gave him a lead, a new link. Indeed, intuitively Isaac the optimist thought that maybe the trip back to Prague held some hope. Perhaps he was now headed in the right direction...

Yisrael Abrams, who had come to Prague to take care of the business of a brother and sister, his clients from New York, and to try and reclaim some of their precious family property in the Jewish Quarter, was eagerly awaiting the next day's meeting with Isaac and Lillian. How surprising and maybe even mystical, he had only known them for a few hours but he already felt connected to them thanks to their fascinating story.

They embraced at the entrance to the Danube Tastes at the designated time. Reserved (and elegant) Lily even kissed Yisrael lightly on the cheek. For her it was an authentic gesture. Yisrael insisted on paying for the meal.
When he heard the name Adv. Peter Jankolovski he couldn't believe his ears. It was the same Czech lawyer and notary whom he himself was using to help regain the property of his clients. They were working together. Only yesterday they had met.

The next morning Adv. Peter Jankolovski introduced Yisrael to his relative, Martina Jatushenko. The proud 94 year old was living in a high-class retirement home in Prague. Yisrael managed to understand from her that she and her husband had hid the little boy Yitzchak and saved his life. For sixty one years she had wondered, until ten years ago together with her husband Alexander, what had happened to the boy whom they had hid and who had later been smuggled by a joint acquaintance to Paris, after the war. Yisrael was astounded.
Yisrael called Isaac and Lillian on their mobile phone and asked them to

come to the retirement home, only 10 minutes from their hotel.
The two came immediately, arriving by cab.

Less than an hour after Peter and Yisrael had arrived at Martina's, six people were sitting with the upright and lucid elderly woman in the well-maintained garden of the high-class retirement home, listening eagerly to her soft and slow but completely rational speech. These were the couple Isaac and Lillian Goldman, Yisrael Abrams, Peter and his wife Marina who worked with him, and Barborba, Martina's daughter.

The noble woman who had rescued Yitzchak Goldman related all the details she knew about Shaul his father and Anya his mother, about how the father taught young children in a small town, and about the mother who was a renowned seamstress in the town. She remembered that his two older brothers and sister were always dressed nicely in clothes sewn for them by their dominant mother. She also remembered the conversations of her husband Adrian with Yitzchak's father, who spoke proudly of his students in the heder. The kind elderly woman of sound mind even described his family home and the giant silver menorah that she remembered despite her old age. She told of how her own son had asked her and her husband to bring Yitzchak home with him to play on that accursed day, when Yitzchak's family was taken from their home by a gang of Ukrainian collaborators.

She continued to describe excitedly how Yitzchak, the little boy, lived with them in secret for about eighteen months until the end of the war. At that time a group of rich American Jews transferred orphans from the Ukraine to France and a short while later took them by ship to the United States. From this stage on Isaac knew what had happened. When he arrived in America he was nearly five years old. He had not known the part about the Ukraine and the short period in Paris. He asked several questions. She answered some of them, and apologized when she did not remember. Isaac Goldman feared that he was overburdening her with his questions. The elderly woman was very excited to relive her memories. He restricted his questions. Her descriptions created for him a picture of his family, his home, and their way of life. He was fortunate to hear quite a few details, considering the length of time that had elapsed and the advanced age of Martina who related, described, and even answered questions. Lillian was tearful. Her loving husband held her hand, their fingers intertwined. Time and again he felt an inner quiver.

Yisrael, who loved stories, thought to himself that no film director could have thought up such a touching human drama. Everyone was very excited and no one got much sleep that night.

The next morning Yisrael, Lillian, and Isaac met at the couple's beautiful hotel. They exchanged impressions of the incredible moving evening. Isaac said excitedly to Yisrael: "The jazz man has linked us. Forever." Isaac was speaking from the heart. Not from the mouth.

Lillian found her courage and asked in a soft voice, "Yisrael, it seems to us that we have known you for a long time, although in fact we know almost nothing about you… only that you are a lawyer from New York, because we focused on my husband's story…"
"Anything you'd like to know about me, just ask…"
"Are you married?"
"No, I'm divorced. I'll be 40 next month. I was only married for a short time. I have no children."
"Maybe you'd be interested in meeting a charming 32 year old woman. Would that be appropriate? She's educated, refined, very pretty. Noble and successful… and she too lives in New York". Lillian paused for a moment and then continued: "I am talking about Julia, our eldest daughter. She too is divorced with no children."
The couple eating with Yisrael at the nice restaurant in the hotel began to fantasize that maybe they would have an ideal son-in-law who together with their daughter would realize their dream and longing to become grandparents.

Isaac and Lillian Goldman were of course not aware of the male sexual preferences of this 'potential ideal son-in-law'. They certainly had no way of knowing, having heard that he had been married in the past, a true fact, although a long time ago.
Yisrael, a handsome man, had got divorced some ten years ago. After being married for two years he suddenly declared his homosexual tendencies. He was much more attracted to men. Since his divorce he had had two lengthy relationships with men.
In the current situation and circumstances he did not wish to expose his tendencies to people to whom he had become so connected, through Isaac's incredible story. He felt that he could not reject their offer but knew that he had to respond without creating unfounded expectations.
"I'd be glad to meet such an attractive woman, particularly if she is your daughter. She must have a special and interesting personality. Certainly, but with no prior agreements this time."

Isaac and Lillian, who had lots of experience in life and even more practical sense, received his response with mixed feelings. They were happy about the possibility and about his eager consent to meet with their daughter, but were disappointed by his reserved reply and his unenthusiastic tone of speech. They had hoped for more but still, there was a chance that maybe…

Yisrael accepted Julia's telephone number in New York and promised to call her once he returned to New York in several days.

And he did.

* * *

Only eleven months had passed since attorney Yisrael Abrams and the Goldmans had happened to meet at the Black Theater in Prague that winter night. The day before the two, Lillian and Isaac, had realized the dream of their life and become grandparents. Their eldest grandson's name was Daniel.

Yisrael Abrams was glad to be a father. He was already in his forties.

Julia Goldman was a happy mother. She knew that the baby, Daniel, would have wonderful genetic qualities inherited from his father Yisrael, a fair and pleasant lawyer.

Nathan, Julia's brother, was happy with his status as an uncle, and his parents stopped pressuring him to get married. They were grandparents already. Julia was very happy that Yisrael had not resisted her parents' suggestion to introduce them.

Julia was also proud of her courage to offer him the 'deal of their life', to have a joint child in their special circumstances.

They began their journey to the birth of their son at the first of their three attempts at sex.

In time, the new father and mother created an outstanding friendship, sharing their most precious asset.

Julia continued to develop her scientific career. The truth was that she did not have much time for suitors. At the same time, she found quality time to devote to Daniel, her charming son. No suitor managed to change her personal status.

Yisrael met a boyfriend, a Czech conductor, with whom he shared his life. Daniel remained, in his words, 'the best thing that had ever happened to him.' Julia, his son's mother, remained his best friend.

Lillian and Isaac were very happy grandparents. The grandfather was reassured, having finally filled the 'black hole' in his past. The grandfather constantly enveloped Daniel, his sweet but naughty grandson, with love, and gave Yisrael all the kind and caring attention he needed.

Daniel made his first trip abroad at the age of five. He and his grandparents were the guests of honor at the 100th birthday celebration of Martina Jatushenko, celebrated at the high-class nursing home 'Life of Joy' in Prague with many guests, including nearly the entire medical and caregiving staff.
At the exciting event Daniel gave Martina a gift sent by his parents, an international bestseller, in its Czech translation:
'The centenarian who climbed out the window and disappeared'…

'Being open is the key to acceptance and development'.

www.ingramcontent.com/pod-product-compliance
Lightning Source LLC
Chambersburg PA
CBHW071201260626
47162CB00003B/1135